FACE TO FACE WITH DEATH!

In a matter of only a few seconds, the man who faced us had himself in hand. I had been on the point of stepping forward to do what I could for his wounded arm, from which the blood had at first freely flowed. But his whole pose was unmistakably one of menace rather than defeat, and the blood-flow ceased almost as abruptly as it had begun, so that I judged it wiser, for the moment at least, to hold my place.

But when the terrible figure spoke to Holmes, it was almost as calmly as before.

"May I congratulate you on thinking of wooden bullets? I had begun to believe all Englishmen were fools."

Also by Fred Saberhagen
published by Tor Books

A Century of Progress
Coils (with Roger Zelazny)
Earth Descended
The Veils of Azlaroc

THE BERSERKER SERIES
Berserker Base
Berserker: Blue Death
The Berserker Throne
The Berserker Wars

THE BOOKS OF SWORDS
The First Book of Swords
The Second Book of Swords
The Third Book of Swords

THE BOOKS OF LOST SWORDS
The First Book of Lost Swords: Woundhealer's Story
The Second Book of Lost Swords: Sightblinder's Story
The Third Book of Lost Swords: Stonecutter's Story
The Fourth Book of Lost Swords: Farslayer's Story

FRED SABERHAGEN

THE HOLMES-DRACULA FILE

A TOM DOHERTY ASSOCIATES BOOK
NEW YORK

This is a work of fiction. All the characters and events portrayed in this
book are fictitious, and any resemblance to real people or events is
purely coincidental.

THE HOLMES-DRACULA FILE

Copyright © 1978 by Fred Saberhagen

Cover art by Glenn Hastings

A Tor Book
Published by Tom Doherty Associates, Inc.
175 Fifth Avenue
New York, N.Y. 10010

Tor ® is a registered trademark of Tom Doherty Associates, Inc.

ISBN: 0-812-52384-9

First Tor edition: September 1989

Printed in the United States of America

0 9 8 7 6 5 4 3

I

There can be little doubt that if the cudgel descending on that old man's skull had been of lead or iron, rather than some stout timber of the English forest, not much would have come of the attempt—at least nothing worthy of your attention and mine at this late date. The street beside the East India docks was very nearly empty in the dawn, and to any assault with mere metal he would have responded vigorously, and then would have gone on his way to meet his love in Exeter, lighthearted with the sense of having done the metropolis of London a good turn *en passant*, ridding it of one or two of its more rascally inhabitants.

It is however an important fact of history—I do not exaggerate—that the force of that stealthy blow, delivered from behind by an assailant of breathtaking cunning, was borne in wood. The old man fell down senseless on the spot; he felt neither the slime of the street's stones nor the rough hands that lifted him and bore him off, their owners doubtless grumbling at his unexpected weight.

There was a great pain in the old man's head when he awoke, and he awoke to nothing better than a crippled awareness, bereft of useful memories. He was in a poor little bedchamber, quite strange to him. And when the old man tried to move, he found that his arms and legs were fettered with iron, held tight to the peculiar high, narrow bed or cot on which he lay. On making this discovery he began, as you may well imagine, very earnestly to consider his situation. But no, he could neither remember nor guess how he might have come to such a pass.

He had no more than shards of memory, all recent but quite incomplete: a sailing ship, a gangplank, the happy feel of solid land beneath his feet once more, the fog-wreathed dawn . . . the great pain in his head.

Now here he was locked to his bed, in a small room he did not know. The lone window was heavily blocked with blinds and curtains, but still admitted more light than he required to take stock of his surroundings. Above it on the stained ceiling a smear of reflected daylight quivered, signaling that water lay outside in the sun. On the far side of the room stood a high old chest of drawers in need of paint, holding on its top an unlit candle in a brass stick, a chipped wash-basin, and a pitcher. A stark chair of dark wood waited inhospitably beside the chest, and that completed the room's furnishings save for the bed itself, which seemed to be fashioned almost entirely of heavy metal.

It might be morning still, or afternoon. The Cockney cries of a coster, hawking vegetables, came from somewhere outside and below. The room, though small, was furnished with two doors, set in adjacent walls. One door was fettered by two closed padlocks, which were large and strong, and mounted upon separate heavy hasps. Little splinters of bright, raw wood about these showed that their installation had been recent. The other door was also closed, but had no lock at all, at least not on the old man's side.

Wafting, oozing from somewhere, was a certain smell. . . .

The pain and damage in his head had left his mind confused and wandering. Yes, a whole symphony of smells was in the city's air. Below and beyond the others was the sea, perceptible to a keen nose though miles away. That and his fragmented memory of being recently aboard ship reminded him that this was London. What was he doing here, so far from home? So far from . . .

Not till his thoughts had reached this point did the old man realize that he no longer knew who he was. If he had been at all susceptible to fear, he would have known it then.

At wrists and ankles, elbows and knees, his arms and legs were clasped to the high, narrow bed by rings of steel, fitted too tightly to leave the smallest chance of wriggling free. When he raised his head as far as possible he could see that his lanky body, still clothed even to elegant frock coat and boots, lay on a sheet of patterned oilcloth. Beneath this, some thin padding covered the hard top and metal frame of this odd cot. It was a sturdy bit of furniture. The old man strained his wiry arms until they quivered, without eliciting so much as a creak from their constraints.

What *was* that smell? Something to do, he thought, with wild animals. With . . .

Footsteps were approaching, outside his room, and he lay back as if no more than semiconscious, and quite too weak to move. Presently the unlocked door was swung in, by a heavyset figure in workman's garb: shabby dirt-colored coat over a gray sweater, baggy trousers, drab cloth cap. Below blue eyes and heavy, blackish brows, most of the man's beefy face was hidden behind a mask of white gauze, held on by strings that looped behind his hairy ears. That mask would look familiar to you now, from films and television if not from direct experience in surgery, but it was strange and puzzling to our old man. In 1897, few people had ever seen the like of it.

'' 'E's awyke, Guv'nor.'' The grating voice that came out through the gauze was addressed to another man not yet in sight, whose steps were drawing near across uncarpeted wood floors. "Plyin' peek with us, 'e is.''

The rough-voiced workman moved aside to let in a much leaner and somewhat taller man, dressed as a gentleman in frock-coat and dark trousers, but masked in the same mysterious style. "So he is,'' this new-comer commented, in an upperclass voice that fit his clothes, and came right over to the waist-high bed. His fair hair was well groomed, and his penetrating blue eyes assessed the old man's condition with a profes-sional economy of movement. With skilled fingers he pressed impersonally about the back of the old man's skull, a region which radiated pain as glowing iron sends out heat. "Hit in the usual spot? Quite. Excel-lently done. No sign of fracture, not even a hematoma. Well, no reason he should not go to the rat at once.''

The old man, who had let his eyelids sag completely shut again, liked to think that in the last few years he had gained a certain facility in English. New bits of slang and jargon, however, continually surprised him. Was "rat,'' in this context, yet another vulgar synonym for latrine? He felt no need for any such facility. In-deed, despite the hurt confusion in his mind, it was for some reason almost amusing to imagine that he might.

The costermonger outside had trundled his leeks into

another street; his voice came faintly now. Within, the two masked insiders, experts enjoying the mystification of their patient, conferred in low and cryptic words. They had turned from his bed and, keys in hand, were rattling open the padlocks upon the little bedroom's second door. It was from behind that door that the smell came, the old man now discovered, the smell of . . . no, it was still impossible for him to think. A hard-wheeled cart assaulted paving stones beneath the window. The cart was being pulled by a big gelded horse whose left front foot felt sore.

Inside the house a third set of human footsteps now drew near. These seemed to be—yes, assuredly they were—the footsteps of a woman, although her shoes clopped the bare floors with authority bold enough for any man. She entered the room, drew near the bed and stopped, and the old man once more cracked an eyelid to observe. She was not large, but held herself erect with the energy of one who lives to dominate. The woman was well dressed in the English style, and it came as no surprise that she should be gauze-masked like the two men.

They must have expected her entrance, for they did not react to it. When the rough-voiced workman had finished taking the locks off the second door, he came over to tie a cloth bag, evidently meant as a blindfold, around the prisoner's head.

The bed, by starting to roll when it was pushed, now proved itself to be a cart. The tall man walked ahead of it, holding open the door that had just been unlocked, while the woman came in the rear, now and then muttering imperious and doubtless unnecessary orders to Rough-voice, on how he should maneuver this strange conveyance into the room adjoining.

Upon the old man's being wheeled into this new chamber, all background smells of the city, the house, the people—in 1897 the modern passion for changing clothes and keeping sterile armpits still had a long way to develop—all common smells, I say, were suddenly wiped out for him, by the sharp tang of carbolic acid. A good deal of this disinfectant was being sprayed and swabbed about. Also the old man's keen ears informed him that his three caretakers were all donning extra clothing. Each was putting a voluminous garment over what he or she already wore.

After these preliminaries had been got through, there proved to be yet another door which must in its turn be unlocked and opened, another threshold to be bumped over on his cart. In this third room, a soft click brought out the unnatural radiance of electric light, perhaps from some kind of handheld torch. Its rays probed at the old man's blindfold and even faintly warmed his exposed hands. All this time he had kept on feigning to be unconscious, largely because in his damaged state he was unable to think of any stratagem more promising. And *now*, despite the steady olfactory roar of the carbolic, there came back, stronger than ever, the animal smell at which he had first wondered.

He could place it now: it was the stink of rodent. Rats, or a rat, but magnified, transformed, intensified. Despite a certain original flavor it was essential Rat, and therefore familiar and unmistakable to that old man, and even almost reassuring. He ought to be able to—to—

To do what? The terrible pain in his head went on, and it was still impossible to think. Impossible to try . . . he did not even know what effort he should try to make.

6

Almost touching his cart, there were more locks and bolts now being operated. These opened no ordinary door, but something that sounded all metal when part of it skreeked back, all metal and full of space as a skeleton.

"Be careful of the screen!" the woman warned. And next moment, the heartbeat and the breathing of a single large inhuman creature were almost within the old man's reach. Here was the radiant center of the rodent smell.

The prisoner's hands began to strain again at their steel restraints, uselessly though with more strength than any victimized old man should have been able to command. But no hunger or rage beat in the animal's heart, so he made his hands relax. Experience counseled waiting, though what experience in his blind past had been remotely like this one he could not guess. Still he felt sure that this was not the first time in his long life that he had been chained and blindfolded. And when the torture started, presently, they would find him no trembling virgin in that field of endeavor either.

Torture? All that came, in apparent anticlimax, was the opening of his clothing at the chest, followed by the pressure there, against his bare skin, of a smooth empty circle like the rim of a glass jar. Inside the circle, a sudden flea crawled on the old man's hide, a tiny timid creature almost frightened by this alien, white and nearly hairless world. Yes, the old man knew it was a flea. He had been for many years a soldier, long ago, and like many another warrior he had become an unwilling connoisseur of vermin. After a moment a second flea came onto his skin, and then by ones and twos additional reinforcements, until he could no longer count the nervous, jumping creatures confined within the circle of the jar. He disliked these creatures, and so he awed them with a great, voiceless, soundless shout, at which command they ceased to jump and huddled in abject obedience.

The glass-rim contact was maintained for several minutes, while the four people in the room were silent. Eventually the woman barked out an order, as if at the conclusion of some timed interval. At this, a thin plate of metal or glass was slid in beneath the glass rim, against the old man's chest and belly. Then cover, jar and fleas were adroitly withdrawn together.

Again locks clashed, and metal bars. In reverse order, doors were opened, the cart was wheeled, carbolic splashed, doors closed, et cetera, and in a few minutes the four human participants were all back in the same room in which the strange charade had started. The old man's blindfold was pulled off by Rough-voice, and this time the old man let his eyes stay open, thinking what the hell or something to that effect. But no one cared if he was wide awake or not. His three tormentors had already turned their backs on him and tramped out. Rough-voice went last, closing the door without padlocks behind him. Before the three began to talk among themselves again they were too many rooms away for the old man to understand a word.

He lay there thinking. To say that he was trying to think would be more accurate. He was still unable to cope with the pain and confusion in his head, the lasting damage of that most savage oaken blow.

Torture, he thought, by fleas. Tickled into trauma by the tripping of their tiny toes. Mangled by their fierce jaws—if he had let them bite. Absurd. Maniacal. But if the intention had not been torture, what? It had all been most deadly serious, in any case.

The blotch of daylight, faint though it was upon the ceiling just above the blinded window, was somehow oppressive to his injured brain. And now his weariness hung like a diver's weights upon his every fettered limb. He could not sleep upon that cart, nor truly rest, but did fall into a kind of trance.

When he came wide awake again it was still full daylight. Again feet were approaching his room's door, the one that had its locks upon the side away from him. With a great clatter it was pushed open, and Rough-voice tramped in, masked as before. His huge hands held a small metal tray bearing a slab of bread, tea steaming in a mug, a glass of water.

With the old man now watching openly, the tray was set down upon a peculiar kind of rest that his brawny keeper snapped up from the bed's right side. Then when the attendant turned a crank somewhere, his aged prisoner's forequarters were elevated, putting him nearly into a sitting position. Rough-voice then brought out a key, and presently one of the manacles restraining the old man's right arm clicked and let go. Now the prisoner could just reach the tray, and might have lifted food and drink from it up to his mouth. He snarled instead and lashed out with a backhanded blow of long-nailed fingers. The tray and its repulsive cargo went splash-and-scatter on the bare floor.

"Ar! Yer a rum cove, ain'cher?" Rough-voice, massive fists on his broad hips, displayed that almost good-humored appreciation not infrequently offered by strong and ruthless people to opposition that is at once spirited and hopelessly weak. "Go dry an' empty then, bein' as you likes it better so!" And with smiling eyes Rough-voice went out by the door where he had entered, not forgetting to re-imprison the old man's wrist.

Outside the room he could be heard squeaking a small, wheeled cart along, and entering one after another a pair of nearby rooms, in each of which his entry was followed by a dull clatter of utensils.

The old man, listening, decided that he shared his captivity with at least two other prisoners. Now that he made the effort, he thought that he could hear their faint and sickly breathing from their separate apartments. Not that he felt any the less alone for the discovery.

Rough-voice moved on with his cart, and now, in yet another room, he paused to make report. "Number One, sir, 'e didn't tyke no water, even."

"Oh?" The responding voice was that of the skillful prober of skulls. "Does he show fever?"

"Not as hi could notice. Didn't touch 'im."

"Quite right. How are the other two?"

"Both given up on shoutin'. Two's eatin, 'three's asleep."

"Very good. Try Number One again in an hour or so. He should eat and drink. And if he's acting strangely, we should have someone with him through the night. His case is not established yet."

"Beg pardon, Guv'nor, but me own orders is t' go out, on that other little job at Barley's. I'll very likely be hangin' around there all night."

"Yes, to be sure." Well-bred vexation in the voice. "Of course there must be no question of deviating from your orders. But it will leave us short-handed."

"There's the girl, Guv'nor."

A little hum of disapproval. Then: "Have you any suggestions?" The question was in a new tone, obviously addressed to someone other than the churlish workman.

It was answered by the woman with the military

walk. "I t'ink we must use the girl." Number One could now discern a stratum of German underneath her cultivated English.

The doctor pondered for a few seconds. "Can we be sure of her?"

"More than uff anyone else we could recruit on such short notice."

"True enough." Another hesitation; then decision. "Yes, we must use her, I suppose. Her reputation is for reliability." Again a switch in his words' aim. "Bring Sally up to keep an eye on Number One tonight. Be sure she stays away from Two and Three; they're too far along to need watching. Impress upon her that she's to stay in the one room, and see that she understands what'll happen to her if she does not hold her tongue about this place."

"Ar."

A door closed, and the voices, already remote and so low that their owners must feel securely private, became too faint for even that old man's ears. He tried to follow them and failed, and then was swamped again by the murderous weariness that only got worse the longer he lay here motionless upon his back. Not cramped or stiff, not even sleepy, but deathly tired. He closed his eyes, and opened them again. This was, he knew, an impossibly wrong place for him to get the rest he craved. But just where would the right place be?

The day wore on. He was not hungry or thirsty. At least—turning his head to glance at the garbage he had knocked to the floor—not for anything like that.

Night crept at last upon the city, and its approach brought to the aged captive at least a partial return of health and strength. The sounds of casual activity that had gone on through the day had faded, and some time had passed in silence, when the old man heard two pairs of feet approaching from a long way off. Shortly Rough-voice walked into the room, a supple, poorly-clad young woman after him. Both of them were masked in gauze.

" 'Ow is it 'e's all bound up like that?'' The voice of the girl bore traces of gentleness, if not concern.

"Told yer, didn't I? 'E's a violent one when 'e gets the chance.'' The man was about to turn and hurry out of the room when he paused in afterthought. " 'Asn't said a bloody word since we got 'im, but that don't mean 'e can't. Might be a real sweet-talker when 'e wants t' be.''

"Won't matter a bit t' me,'' the girl said lightly. And like the visiting nurse she parked a cloth bag that she was carrying atop the tall chest of drawers, and looked about her for a place to settle. There was only the one hard chair.

"See that it don't. Well, then, I'm off.''

"Ah.'' It was almost the man's *ar*.

Rough-voice shut the door behind him. His tread receded, went jauntily bouncing down some distant stairs.

Left alone with the old man, the young girl turned to size him up more thoroughly. Her eyes were brown and hard, fragments of London cobblestone above the border of her white mask, whose strings where they went back to her ears were hidden by brown curls. The sun was setting now, and the room had grown much darker in the last few minutes, but in keeping with all the other seeming perversities of his situation, the old man only saw her all the better for the failing of daylight. Her dress was coarse and plain and patched, and he thought that the scarf she draped on the chair's back would have been better suited to a man.

"Well," she said, and came over to stand beside his bed, looking at the floor. "A pretty mess you've made. And none o' them'd ever think of cleaning up, of course."

Sally. But the name could be a weapon, the only weapon he had, and he must wait for the proper time to strike with it.

"Release me," the old man told her suddenly, his voice so deep and firm that it surprised himself. "And I will clean up what I have spilled." To have begun with something that sounded like cleverness would surely have put a clever girl on guard.

"Well, well, 'e talks! And like a bloody toff. Dressed like 'un, too." But still Sally hardly looked at the old man, as she bent to pick up the spilled refuse. The stain from the tea was large, yet scarcely conspicuous on worn floorboards long since abandoned to their fate. Bread, mug, glass and tray the girl carried to some outer room, whence sounded a dull clatter of utensils. She came back in a minute, chewing on something, and stood before him with folded arms as if to ask him silently: How am I to stand your company for hours and hours?

On his part hoping for long hours of isolate companionship, the old man spoke again, letting his voice take on a certain sound of stagy tragedy. "No, girl, I was quite wrong to ask you to release me. If there be more chains you can add, I bid you bring them here and lock them on." He was not one for thinking through his plans with any complete logic; perhaps he tried this zig-zag tactic on the chance that the girl would feel she ought to do the opposite of anything he urged her. Well, he was still half-addled.

Whatever Sally might have felt, she did not sound surprised. "Don't 'ave no more chains. Do 'ave some scrag I might bring in, if you'll promise not t' fling it all about this time."

He let his voice sag down to being weakly friendly. "I promise that."

"I'll myke some tea." Coolly practical, she left the door ajar and went off to what must have been the kitchen. In the middle distance he could hear her, now pouring water, now cutting bread. Now came the subtle sound of a knifeblade spreading out a heap of jam. His imagination's picture of the rich red stuff brought on a wave of hunger, mixed with a little nausea.

The irrelevant smell of tea soon took form on the night air. The old man strained his limbs again and then lay back, unable to budge his iron bonds, hissing his exhaustion. Good God but they were strong. Had this bed-cart been constructed to confine a mad gorilla?

Here Sally came back to him, replenished tea-tray in her hands. It was now so dark that she must grope her way, and she had removed her mask, which must have been an annoyance to keep on for hours and hours. The old man could now plainly see her face, which would have been pretty were it not for a great birthmark, covering her whole right cheek and jaw, more strawberry than the stuff which she had spread upon the bread—and were it not, of course, for the corollary of this disfigurement, a set of resignation in all her facial muscles, the look of bitter, sullen surrender to all the world's foul ugliness.

She felt secure, of course, that in this lightless room

he'd never see her face. Meanwhile he watched the innate and unconscious grace with which, even unable to see the way, she moved across the room.

" 'Ere. Can you see it?'' She put the tray down where it had been before, upon the stand that branched out from the bed.

"My hand could find it in the dark. Alas, I cannot move a finger.''

Sally went away and groped for the stiff chair and brought it back, sat down in it an arm's length distant. Perhaps I have exaggerated the room's darkness; there must have existed a little ghost of light, oozing from the shaded window at her back, to fall across his bed. No doubt she could see him at least faintly, while believing that her own face was fully hidden from his eyes.

She tore off a morsel of the bread and held it toward his lips. " 'Ere. It's crusty, but you 'as a good mouthful o' teeth for an old 'un. I could see that when you first spoke t' me.''

His neck muscles reflexively turned his head away. It was not red jam that he hungered for. "I thank you deeply, but I find I cannot eat.''

"Ah.'' There was again some gentleness in her voice. Sally popped the morsel into her own mouth. "Want some tea?'' She spoke as one who does not wish to dine alone.

"Where am I, girl?''

"You've 'ad a knock on the 'ead, you 'ave. So you're—in 'ospital.''

"But in what city?'' Although of that, at least, he had no doubt.

"How 'bout some tea: 'Spect I'll have it meself if you won't.''

"Thank you, but no. Some water, if you please," he added, so he should not seem too strange. With water his old guts could cope, he felt.

"Right-o." She held the glass for him, while being careful, he noted, to touch neither his gray lank hair that straggled before his face, nor his clothing, nor his skin. He managed to raise his head enough to drink whilst his arms stayed bound down. Water slid toward his stomach, where it lay unabsorbed, like liquid glass.

"Girl . . ." He lay back, blowing through wet lips. "What shall I call you?"

"Never you mind." Then there occurred a thought that pleased her privately. "You can call me 'Miss.' "

"Miss. Will you then be kind enough to tell an old man why he is being held a prisoner?" Night deepened; he was waking up. The words had begun to dance along naturally, without thought on the old man's part. The finger-movements of a violinist, tuning a new instrument, whose hands over the long, long years have cradled a thousand others like it.

"I told you, yer in 'ospital." Making herself cold and abrupt was not something that came naturally to Sally. She had practiced for enough years, though, to do it well. She could be ruthless. Now she was eating, quite neatly, the rest of the bread and jam he had refused.

"Miss. Please." The old man played for pity. She could be ruthless but it did not suit her, and he supposed he must look shriveled and senile as he lay bound before her. Her own dear father was somewhere tonight . . . but one had to be careful along that route. Across the room the cracked fragment of a mirror leaned upon a high shelf close to the chest of drawers, but the angle was wrong for him to be able to see himself in it. Besides . . .

Besides what? Something important had come and gone before he could grasp it. So much was gone, so much remaining was now jumbled, broken, useless, inside this savage persisting pain that felt as if it must deform his head. Anyhow she had called him old, and there was his gray hair twisting before his eyes. And he could see his own hands, and thought that they looked old. Wrinkled and gray-furred on the backs, yes, old-looking despite the strong long nails and the incongruous firm plumpness of the palms that so contrasted with the leanness of his wrists where they emerged from newly dirty cuffs.

"Why am I shackled, Miss? I have done no one any harm."

"You gets violent at times. Out 'o yer 'ead, so t' speak. That's why you 'as t' be restrained a bit." She had a relish for the jam that she was finishing, but not for lies.

He would now strike with the name, and see what magic wound he might inflict. "I hope devoutly, Sally, that . . ."

Right in the heart. She jumped up, chair almost toppling back, breadcrumbs scattering to the floor. " 'Ow'd you know my *nyme?*"

"Ah, my dear girl! I did not realize that *your* name was a secret, too. Do you know mine? It has been taken from me." Which was the all-too-painful truth.

Her face hung over him. Her fists were clenched. " 'Ow'd you *know?*"

He had seen and heard far too many real menaces to take this one very seriously. Her anger was not aimed at

17

him, of course. "My dear . . . I had no wish to upset you. You have been kind to me. The others mentioned your name, with some laughter . . . as if there were some joke. But then, perhaps I am mistaken."

"Joke? Tell me wot joke!" She leaned over him, still trying to sound threatening. But one hand was now raised to conceal her disfigurement, in case the dark should fail her at close range.

"Perhaps I am mistaken, as I said. Perhaps, for all I know, it is mere accident that yours is the only name my caretakers have spoken freely. There is no reason, is there, why the names of my attendants should be secret?"

"Ow, damn them!" Sally fell back into her chair, muttering to herself, and perhaps not hearing the old man at the moment. "*Damn* all their ber-luddy eyes!"

"And the names of the doctor in charge, and his good wife?"

That caught Sally's attention back, and for a moment it seemed she might be going to utter a harsh laugh. "Huh! Wife? Not 'er!" Then the girl retreated abruptly into a silence so quick and accomplished that it must have been an habitual defense.

Now wait, the old man told himself. Wait for a little while before you push again. His brain still throbbed, distracting him with pain, refusing to yield his rightful memories. How could he plan or act? Yet he must do the best he could.

Presently, in this deep night that was to his eyes clear as brightest day, the girl got up and moved about the room. Standing for a moment by the window, she pulled the curtain back for a furtive, nervous peek, looking out blankly, not as if she really expected to see anything of importance. Then she went to the tall chest of drawers, fondled the candle in its holder for a moment, and put it down again. Next with decisive steps she left the room, to come back shortly, once more masked, and carrying a lighted oil lamp which she set on the tall chest. She moved the chair back closer to the light and, somewhat to the old man's surprise, extracted from her bag a small book. This she settled down to read.

"What are you reading, Sally?" Though he could see the faded printing on the cover: Christina Rossetti's *Goblin Fair*.

She raised her eyes to his some seconds before answering. "A long poem, like. A lady wrote it." She told him what the title was.

"And are the goblins in it terrible?"

"Oh, no sir." The "sir" seemed quite unconscious. "Least *I* don't think they are." Sally was on the verge of confiding more, but changed her mind, blanked her face, and dropped her eyes back to the safety of the printed page. She read with an occasional lip-movement, but well enough for all that, to judge from the deft shuttling of her eyes. Outside, the night was growing darker, and there came a hint of ozone in the air, even before the old man could hear the distant thunder. Still faintly audible were the two sets of his fellow prisoners' lungs, in nearby rooms—they sounded like two old men slowly dying.

"The word 'goblin,' " he remarked, "derives I believe from the Greek *kobalos*, and means 'rogue.' "

"Ah." Above Sal's mask her eyes came back to fasten on his face, as if unwillingly.

"How old are you, Sally?"

"Turned seventeen last Easter. Look 'ere sir, you sure you don't want no tea?"

"Quite sure."

"And they spoke out my name, hey?" The book went down in her lap. "Wot'd they say?"

"Very little."

"Come on, wot?"

"That you were to stay with me, tonight." His voice was low and tired and patient. "And there was some indelicacy, which I should prefer not to repeat. And something, somehow, amused them—having a connection with your appearance, perhaps; I could not hear them clearly. I say, is there anything wrong? I'm sorry."

She had frozen in her chair, and under her mask there might now be a ghastly kind of smile. I have not said he was a kindly, good, benevolent old man.

At last the thunder of the approaching storm rolled near enough for her to hear it, and broke in upon her poisoned reverie. She glanced at the closed window, then back at the old man. And then back to her book.

He let her turn two pages. Then: "Sally, what lies behind that door?" When the girl looked up he indicated with a movement of his head the doubly padlocked portal.

"Ah, just some drugs an' medicines an' things." She was making up an answer to avoid being bothered by the question. Her deeper thoughts were elsewhere—without doubt, still brooding upon those vicious employers of hers who laughed at her blotched face. Now, how could she get back at them? Oh, he was not a considerate, truthful old man at all. But long-lived, yes indeed.

He asked: "No living thing is kept in there?"

She put her book down in her lap again, forefinger holding place. "Why, barrin' a mouse or a bug or two,

I don't s'pose there's any. *Kept*, you say? Wot kind o' livin' thing?"

"Go listen at the door." The thunder grumbled closer. The giant Rat liked not the coming storm, and in between its atmospheric slams and rumbles the prisoner now and again perceived a huffing squeal that issued from no human throat.

Sally automatically started to get up, as if to do what the old man had bidden her. Then she caught herself. "Ahh, it's the storm you're hearin'," she decided, and sat down. Still, in doing so, she unconsciously hitched her chair a little closer to the old man, though this caused the light to fall more dimly on her book.

Next time the thunder came he could hear, beneath her patched dress, the life pump more quickly through young veins and arteries. He thought: *Look up*, and her eyes lifted and were caught on his.

Ah, that old man could hypnotize, sometimes. But his broken memory made him uncertain of himself, and his powers of concentration were flawed by injury. More important, this particular young girl was quite reluctant to deliver her own will completely to another. She might have fought free of the softest, most enticing web he could have woven on his best day.

Still, in some corner of her heart, she must have welcomed this approach so much like wooing—even as, with a shake of her head, she spurned it. "Look 'ere, lemme get you another drink at least."

"That would be kind." And while she was out, this time, he turned his head and regurgitated, in a clear stream that vanished into the visual mosaic of that experienced floor, the small amount of water he had swallowed earlier.

This movement of his head, with neck stretched out

as much as he could manage, dislocated the poor oilcloth pad from under his bruised skull. Sally's first instinct when she returned to him was to reach out and set this right; and when she leaned over the old man, his mind was dazzled by the soft throbbing in her slender throat of the great vessels there that tinged the fair skin blue above them.

She put the pad straight, and then remembered orders and stood back a step. "I wasn't to touch you, not your bed even. Very firm on that point, 'e was, and I shouldn't be surprised if 'e should 'ave some means o' tellin'."

"I would never betray one who sought to help me."

She stood there without answering, and held the glass of water for him as before.

He drank, as if it were a great boon, and lay back exhausted by the effort. "Thank you."

"Ah well. Now I s'pose I could hand yer the bedpan or bottle if y'wish. I've done a bit o' nursin' in me time."

"No thank you, Sally." He paused to look at her with yearning concentration. "You do have the kind hands of a nurse, I see. The body of a good graceful dancer. And that mask cannot hide your beauty from me."

"Ar," she said, and started looking round to see where she had left her book. She was quite good at not letting any feelings show. More than a decade she must have practiced that, since first she looked into a mirror with understanding.

"Of course I do not know your face. But what I mean is, even if you had no face at all, or if your face were far from what the world calls pretty, yet when I saw it your beauty would be just the same, unmarred for me."

Sally hardly hesitated as she turned away and went to where her book lay on the chair. The rain roared suddenly upon the nearby roofs. He let his tensed neck-sinews soften; his head lolled back upon the pad that she had straightened for him. Why oilcloth? Easy to clean? But nobody cared about that, as a rule.

And somewhere in his upper jaw a faintly delicious aching had begun. To be precise, the ache lay at two points, the toothroots of his canines. But the continuing skull pain soon squashed this interesting sensation jealously out of perception's range, continuing to hold for itself the center of the stage.

"I wish I had my memory intact," he said. "Then I could tell you the name of that great beauty . . . a certain girl I knew when I was young, who is recalled to me when I behold your youth and grace."

"Oh, sir." What with one thing and another, he had her upset now, enough so that she gave up trying to conceal it. Dismayed, angered, delighted all at once. She must have been aware with one part of her mind that he was telling her some wild tales, but she was greatly taken with them all the same.

The violinist's fingers warmed and flew. If his old brain had not been quite so traumatized, he could have found the precise words, the exactly right expression. The girl and victory should have been his, in full, before the muddy dawn came round. But as true history went, he had some fuddled moments, in which he lost his best line of attack. Unable to put off wondering who he was, he said to her: "Has none of them ever spoken my name in front of you?"

"No sir. I doubt they knows your name." Then she feared that she had said more than was prudent.

"Sally. If this unjust, cruel imprisonment must end

in my death—if it must, then let it be my heart's last wish, that my eyes may behold your beauty near me, as they close." Oh yes, I know. But really it was not the words he said so much as the way he said them; nor even the way the old man said them, so much as the hunger of the girl who listened. And at the time and place of which I write, real men and women really entreated one another in these and similar terms. People were moved by words like these to weep real tears—as Sally wept that night, before the dawn. In the late twenty-first century we all—all of us who are still quick above the ground—shall marvel at the styles of speech and writing that we admired back in the twentieth.

"Sally, the keys."

"Oh, sir, I 'aven't got them, on my soul."

"But you know where they are."

"Oh, sir, I daren't even think of that. God, no!"

His head hurt, hurt, hurt. The storm blew past, the short hours of the summer night dragged with it. In inner thought, beneath his saintly victim's mask, he raged at the poor bedeviled girl who could not quite make up her mind.

Time was running out on that old man. "They mean to kill me, girl." It was a statement bald and true.

Books and all else forgotten, she alternately huddled in the chair and paced the floor. "*I* don't know *that*, sir. I *do* know wot they'll do t' me should I do aught to cross 'em. Lord!"

The little strength and wit that he had left were failing. Dawn was near, time running, running out. He heard the four-wheeler coming along the otherwise deserted street. He heard it long before Sally did, yet there was nothing more that he could do.

II

(This and succeeding alternate chapters are from a manuscript in the handwriting of the late John H. Watson, M.D.)

It is with emotions doubly strange that I at last take up my pen to write the story involving the creature I have elsewhere referred to as the Giant Rat of Sumatra—a story, I may add, that until quite recently I had thought likely would remain forever unrecorded.

My feelings are strange because, in the first place, this was surely the most bizarre case in all the long and illustrious career of my friend Sherlock Holmes. God knows the creature I have called the Rat was peculiar enough in itself; but the case also involved a truly monumental crime. And it was made unique by the glimpse it offered into an incredible world, whose existence I had never before suspected, a world of horror seemingly more than mortal, but coexisting with the staid, humdrum life of Victorian London. I must admit here in passing, that in this terrible year of 1916 in which I write, that apparently stable pre-war world is almost as difficult to believe in as the world which the adventure of the Rat discovered. That 19th-century London, and that Europe, have long since died upon the battlefields of France.

In the second place, besides the grotesque and terrible nature of the adventure itself, there is the strange fact that what I write is not, in this case, to be placed immediately before the public. It is even probable that both Holmes and I will have been for some years beyond the reach of all this world's concerns, before these lines are allowed to see the light of day.

"There are more things in heaven and earth, Watson . . ." Holmes mused, recently, as I was visiting him at his retirement home in Sussex. "Yes, I think you must write about the Rat, for the benefit of others who will come after us. But what you write must not be read this year, or probably for some years to come; and you must change the names of those involved, wherever prudence suggests such alteration."

"As to altering names, Holmes, I have done as much in detailing some of your other cases. But if it is not to be published in the near future, then when? And who is to decide?"

"Well, there is one man, I believe, whom we can trust to see to it that the story is placed before the public when the time is ripe, and not before."

"Holmes—" I began a protest.

"Yes, Watson, I know your views." He looked at me severely for a moment. Then his gaze softened. "I shall handle the necessary arrangements. Believe me, old fellow, it will be for the best. Therefore you must go home and write."

And so it is that I am now seated at my desk. When complete, this account will not be entrusted to my own depository of confidential papers, Cox's bank at Charing Cross, where lie the unfleshed bones of many another remarkable tale. Rather, by Holmes' own instructions, it must go with some few private papers of his own, into the deepest vaults of the Oxford Street branch of the Capital and Counties bank. There it is to remain for years or decades, for centuries if need be, until a most singular password shall be presented for its removal.

The adventure began for me upon a sunny morning in early June of 1897. London was in a bustle of preparation for the Jubilee, and thronged with important visitors from every quarter of the Empire. The early months of that year had been an extremely busy time for Holmes as well, so arduous in fact that in March he had been ordered to rest, and I had accompanied him to Cornwall, where occurred those remarkable events I have recorded elsewhere as the Adventure of the Devil's Foot.

On this morning I found Holmes at breakfast, turning over in his hands a small blue envelope. "I have not mentioned this to you yet, have I, Watson?" he exclaimed by way of greeting. "If not, it is only because in the press of recent events I have not found time, either to discuss it or to give it the full attention it perhaps deserves."

"An appeal from a lady, no doubt," I commented, taking my chair.

"Really, Watson, you outdo yourself. Yes, the feminine handwriting of the address will admit of no other interpretation. It is in fact a rather distraught young American lady, a Miss Sarah Tarlton, and this is the third communication I have received from her. The first was a cable from New York, and the second a packet of letters and a note sent yesterday afternoon, just after she arrived in London. She is coming here in person in half an hour, and I will be pleased if you would remain."

"Certainly, Holmes, if there is anything I can do."

"You can listen, old fellow. You are an invaluable listener. While we wait, I may perhaps outline for you her problem, as her successive written messages have presented it to me."

"I am all ears."

Holmes had finished his own breakfast, and while I attacked mine he pushed back his chair and lighted his first pipe of the day. "Miss Tarlton," he began, "comes from a good family in New York. Her father is an eminent member of the medical profession there, and I suppose it is quite natural that she should have bestowed her heart upon another physician, Dr. John Scott. A very brilliant young man, by his fiancee's account at least, and evidently determined to prove himself.

"Young Scott's talents lie—or lay; it is uncertain whether he is still alive—chiefly in research aimed at discovering the chemical and biological agents of disease. His studies in the laboratory were praised, but could not be conclusive in finding the cure he sought. Having some means of his own, and acquiring financial aid from other sources, he outfitted an expedition to the East Indies, where pestilential death is likely to be found at home to any caller.

"His departure took place just two years ago, in June of 1895. It was the agreement that upon his return to New York, having, as he expected, achieved success in his dangerous researches, he and Miss Tarlton should marry.

"For more than a year he wrote her faithfully, and she of course responded. The irregularity of the post sometimes brought her several letters from him at once, and twice months passed without a word. Therefore her alarm was not instantaneous when the young man disappeared.''

"You mean—?''

"I mean he ceased to write, or at any rate his letters ceased to arrive in America. After five months had passed with no word, Miss Tarlton began to find more and more ominous certain hints of danger appearing in his last letters. Her attempts to communicate with the American embassies and consulates nearest to his last known whereabouts in Sumatra produced no helpful information. More months passed and the young lady grew increasingly worried. She and her father were on the point of organizing a search expedition, when something happened that turned her attention halfway across the world. Her young man, or so there is some reason to believe, has recently been seen alive and well in London.''

"London! But why on earth should he have come here?''

"There is no apparent reason. And from all that I have yet learned of his character, Watson, it rings false that he should act in a deliberately callous way to his betrothed.''

"What was the nature of his research?'' I moved my plate away, and began filling my own pipe.

"Well, word had reached him in America that the disease for which he sought a cure was endemic in certain remote parts of the interior of Sumatra. His letters from that island to Miss Tarlton describe its strange pattern of infection in those regions. Village after village was ravaged, in a slow geographical progression suggesting the movement through the jungle of a single causative agent, perhaps a living creature of some kind.

"Such reports as he had from the natives insisted that this agent was in fact a large animal—some claimed it to be an orangutan, the great ape of the region; others spoke of a large rodent, a kind of monstrous rat."

"Good heavens, Holmes!"

"Young Scott's letters—I have them here, and you can read them later—detail his pursuit of this animal under conditions of extreme difficulty and hardship. The sole companion who had set out with him from America, another young scientist, fell ill with fever early in the game and had to return home. But Scott persevered, using native assistants. He of course faced danger from tropic diseases, from the natural obstacles of the uncharted wilderness, from beasts, and from some of the island's more savage inhabitants. And in his last letter there is a hint of still another kind of trouble—he mentions the presence, within a few miles of his own camp, of some European expedition."

"I should have thought he'd find the presence of other civilized men very welcome."

"So he did, evidently. And yet . . . well, it would be a waste of time to theorize on those far-off events with no more data than are yet on hand. And here, unless I am mistaken, is Miss Tarlton herself, and you will be able to hear the details from her own lips."

A moment later the lady was shown in. Few visitors more lovely can ever have crossed our threshold. She was richly but very modestly dressed. Her blue eyes at first glance searched me with hope, almost with pleading, as if I might represent some answer to her prayers. But when we were introduced, the hope in her gaze quickly faded, to be reborn an instant later as she turned to my companion. "Mr. Holmes. I am told that if any living person can solve my problem, you are that man.''

"Pray sit down, Miss Tarlton. I am eager to hear in some greater detail the facts as you have outlined them in your letters. In particular, exactly when, and under what circumstances, was your fiance identified in London? What makes you so sure that it was he?''

Greatly agitated, the lady leaned forward in the chair she had just taken. "Mr. Holmes, I *can't* be sure." She drew a deep breath. "It happened this way. A mutual friend of John's and mine, Mr. Peter Moore, happened to be on business in this city last month, when he received a call from the London firm of Morrison, Morrison, and Dodd, who I understand are specialists in assessing machinery. The ship *Matilda Briggs*, bound for Portsmouth from the South Seas, had run aground upon the Eddystone Rocks. The salvors brought much of the cargo on to London. In it, some peculiar items had turned up, evidently of American manufacture; Mr. Moore was known to be the owner of an American firm that builds medical and laboratory equipment, and by good fortune he was in London; would he be kind enough to give an opinion on the goods?

"He agreed. Then he was naturally very surprised when he arrived at the warehouse and found the very equipment, most of it still intact, that John had purchased from him for the Sumatran expedition.

"Peter's first impulse was to cable me. But he didn't know that John had been so long unreported, and he was afraid of frightening me. He decided to try to learn, first, who the things now belong to, and why they had been aboard the *Matilda Briggs*. Was John in England, too? The people at the warehouse could be of no more help than to say that the material did seem to belong to a Dr. John Scott of New York. Nor could Morrison, Morrison, and Dodd provide any more information.

"His own business kept Peter occupied for a day or two. Then he went back to the warehouse, intending to complete his inspection of the equipment and write out a report for the assessors. He was greatly surprised to find that every bit of the material in question had been claimed, signed for and paid for, and already removed, apparently by John himself."

"One moment, Miss Tarlton," Holmes interposed. "Has Dr. Scott actually been seen in London by Peter Moore? Or by anyone who knows him well?"

"He has not. But the superintendent of the warehouse describes the man who claimed the equipment as blond, tall—John is tall, about the same height as you are, Mr. Holmes—with a narrow face and a thick mustache. All this fits very well. Here is the photograph I promised to bring. It shows John just a few days before leaving for Sumatra."

The small picture showed an eager, manly face, smiling and squinting a trifle in bright sunshine.

"This is a good likeness?" Holmes asked.

"Yes, very good, so I believe."

He put it into his pocket. "Now, the man who came to the warehouse of course presented identification? And he must have left there at least one copy of his signature."

"He did. The men at the warehouse insist that he presented them with letters of credit bearing John's name, with—oh, with a mass of documents, evidently. And he described the equipment he was claiming in such detail, even to the crates that it was packed in, that those in charge were fully satisfied of his identity." Miss Tarlton sighed, and the weariness behind her energy showed through. "There was also the matter of—I think they called it salvage money—and of storage charges, and I don't know what other fees. This came to almost five hundred pounds, which sum I understand was paid all at once, in cash. As to the man's signature, they would not give me a counterfoil, but I was permitted to see it." Here our lovely visitor hesitated.

"Yes?" Holmes prompted.

"It was John's name, of course, and the writing was quite similar to his. But *I* do not believe that it was written by his hand."

"Have you been to the police?" I asked.

"I have, Dr. Watson. We—Peter Moore and I— went to Scotland Yard yesterday, as soon as I had checked into a hotel. The gentlemen there were sympathetic, and they assured me that some inquiries will be made. But I did not get the impression that they are going to push an investigation with the urgency that is required. There is, as they told me so soothingly, no real evidence of any crime. No doubt they have a thousand other urgent problems demanding their attention . . . no doubt you, too, Mr. Holmes, are a very busy man. And yet I dare to—to demand your help. I am prepared to pay handsomely for it. I feel that you are my only hope!"

This last sentence was delivered in tones so brave and yet so piteous that I had little doubt of what Holmes' answer must be. Nor was I disappointed.

"I will undertake to look into your problem, Miss

Tarlton,'' my friend replied. ''The man who signed the goods out of the warehouse must have given some London address?''

''Yes, Mr. Holmes; the Northumberland Hotel. I was there inquiring, with Peter, just this morning. No John Scott was presently registered. I pursued my inquiries no further, but instead waited till I could see you.''

''In that you acted wisely.'' Holmes rose casually, went to the window, and stood there for a few seconds almost as if daydreaming. Then he gave his head a little shake. Miss Tarlton I suppose read little or nothing into these actions, but I knew from long experience that he had just surveyed Baker Street for anyone who might be watching our house, and had observed nothing suspicious.

My friend came back to us. ''I must warn you, Miss Tarlton, that I foresee no great probability of a happy outcome in this case.''

Her chin lifted. ''I am determined to find out the truth.''

''And there is something I must ask you at the outset: Had you written angrily to your fiance? Or had there been any suggestion, on either side, of breaking the engagement?''

The girl stood up, color flushing her cheeks. Her blue eyes flashed. ''No, Mr. Holmes, to both questions. I have given you copies of all John's letters, which I believe spoke his true feelings. On my part—I would rather have died than cease to love him. If you mean to imply that John has willingly abandoned me, without a word, without a letter of explanation, I simply refuse to believe it. He may be dead, in shipwreck or by some other means. He may have suffered some terrible loss of memory . . ."

She could not go on, and Sherlock Holmes took her reassuringly by the hand. "You can leave the burden of the mystery in our hands now, Miss Tarlton. I have every confidence that we shall be able to find the man who signed John Scott's name, if he is still in England; and when we have found him, I shall be very much mistaken if further answers do not come within our grasp."

"Mr. Holmes, my gratitude is—I am forever in your debt." Then, recovering somewhat, our visitor reached again into her handbag, from which she had produced the photograph. "I have here the list, which Peter has given me, of the equipment—or as much of it as he had time to examine."

She handed over several folded sheets of paper, which Holmes opened and glanced at before sending Miss Tarlton back to her hotel, which a repetition of such reassurance as he could honestly give. When she had gone, he looked at the papers again, before holding them out in my direction. "Rather bizarre . . . perhaps somewhat in your line, Watson. What do you make of it?"

I took the papers and studied them briefly. "An unusual line of research, certainly." Among a hundred or so items listed were not only the usual laboratory paraphernalia that any chemical or medical scientist might have employed, but also numbers of iron fetters of various shapes and sizes, collapsible cages (some very large), along with operating tables, beds, and treatment and examination tables sufficient to have equipped the infirmary of a zoo, or perhaps a small hospital. Some of these beds and tables were provided, in the words of Peter Moore, with "steel restraints, and suited for experiments on any of the great apes, or creatures of comparable size and strength."

I commented: "It seems he had equipped himself well for the pursuit of the animal, whether ape or rodent. Did he ever find it?"

"He did. The facts are in the letters."

"And the disease organism, Holmes, upon which all this investigative effort was to center? I do not believe Miss Tarlton told us that."

"She had informed me of that detail in an earlier communication. It was *Pasteurella pestis*, Watson. Plague."

III

Sally could not hear the four-wheeler approaching two streets away, but when it arrived, with a clash of iron wheelrims against the curb, she heard and jumped up from her chair. It was as if those who controlled her life and the prisoner's had already detected her in the betrayal that she had dared to dream about for one dread, glorious moment. Then the sudden terror faded from her eyes, to be replaced by a mixture of relief and agonized sympathy for the old man. But without another word to him she gathered her things and fled the room, pausing at the door to cast back a piteous glance that seemed to beg for his forgiveness.

Bah.

Spent by his long, fruitless efforts at seduction, and enervated by the return of daylight, the old man endured his ceaselessly throbbing head and listened. Several rooms away, the cultured voice of the doctor, newly arrived, was probing at Sally, who gave him hasty, fearful answers. The prisoner could hear the tones though not the words of both their voices. He heard also faint morning stirrings from his two fellow prisoners in their nearby rooms. Presently Sally's feet went rapidly downstairs. A street door opened and shut behind her; the sound of her steps on the pavement dwindled and disappeared.

Soon afterward the doctor began on his brief morning rounds. He came to the old man's room freshly redolent of carbolic acid, and this time wearing a surgeon's gown, which in that year was as much of an innovation as the mask.

"Well, sir, I perceive that you are unequivocally awake this morning, which we must count as progress, I suppose." As he offered this dubious greeting, the doctor's machine-like hands, today in fine rubber gloves, were palming the victim's forehead in search of fever that was not there, palpating the gaunt abdomen, turning back an eyelid.

Not far behind the doctor came the harsh clop of the hard woman's boots. Her face, like his covered up to the eyes in gauze, looked round his gowned shoulder. "Any signs yet?" she inquired.

"No. But the incubation period may be as long as ten days, remember."

"Vell then, hardly to be expected yet."

The old man let his gaze drift vacantly away from the two faces, then brought it back to focus on them as if with a great effort.

The two exchanged a few more words, then began to strip their victim, cutting away his expensive clothing ruthlessly, dropping it into a cloth bag. Only now, after he had been their captive for so long, were his pockets searched and his papers examined, by two gauzed heads posed briefly side by side.

"If the name's Corday," the woman offered, "the nationality is likely French."

"I suppose so. He took ship at Marseilles, I see." Not that it really mattered to them; they were satisfying a passing curiosity. Then they garbed the old man in a kind of hospital shirt or gown of tight-woven fabric, fastening the sleeves upon his arms with small cloth ties.

Corday, he thought. Marseilles. The words meant *something* personal to the old man. Or at least he felt they should have done. The name of the city brought up a hazy recollection of its skyline as seen from the Vieux Port. But Corday was not the old man's true name, of that much he was certain; nor was French his native tongue, though he could speak it fairly well.

A stethoscope had appeared. The old man was enjoined—in awkward French, this time—to breathe more deeply. He obediently made the front of his rib cage move up and down.

The doctor spoke in English, half amused, half puzzled. "Monsieur Corday, your respiration's very shallow, almost undetectable. Heartbeat is strong, but—" He shook his head, mystified. He felt the old man in the armpits and in the groin. Then he said to the woman: "I must take a blood sample."

"Ve must not spend too much time on this particular case. There are others to be tested. Results will be required of us, not specimens and theories."

"A blood sample is necessary, in my opinion. We cannot produce good results without knowledge."

The woman turned silently away. She was back shortly with a glass syringe that gleamed with sharpness.

Two attempts upon the inner elbow of the old man's right arm, where one vein stood up prominently, brought about a broken steel needle and some upper-class profanity. A new needle was obtained and the assault renewed. At last a trickle of red crawled into a glass tube. Meanwhile familiar heavy feet had been climbing the stair from the outside world. Their owner, masked but not gowned, came upon the scene just in time to witness this small success.

"Ah, you're back," the doctor welcomed Rough-voice. "What luck?"

"On'y indifferent, Guv'nor. Which is to say Barley ain't got quite the numbers nor the quality we wants, as yet. But 'e 'as 'opes. Wot's up 'ere?"

"Hopes, has he? Our time is not unlimited. The twenty-second of June draws near. Well, we shall discuss that presently. Have you slept?"

"Ar." The workmen stretched his powerful frame, arms over head. "Could do wi' a cuppa tea and bit o' scrag, though."

"Well, before you breakfast, do have another word with the girl. I believe things went well enough here through the night, but best make sure. She seemed rather to have the wind up when we came in this morning."

"Ar."

Small glass-tubed sample of gore in hand, the doctor led the others from the room, meanwhile continuing their conversation. "And try to feed this one again when you get back; she said he took nothing but water. We want to maintain some strength in him to obtain a valid result. But mind you don't touch him, or his bed."

"Wotcher think, I'm goin' ter do that?" The door closed and they were gone.

In a few minutes the doctor was back, a fresh hypodermic in hand. Above his mask he scowled at the old man as if insulted by him, and stabbed at him for more blood. The doctor did not believe what his microscope had just informed him regarding the first sample.

Another needle splintered, a circumstance that the physician dismissed with no more than an impatient oath. No giant of research, he, to pounce upon this apparently small but truly significant phenomenon. Of course it might be claimed in his defense that he labored amid dangers and distractions notably absent from the ordinary laboratory. And there was no room in his thoughts for any truly great discovery, for they were fully occupied with the preparation of an equally great crime.

A new needle was made to work, after a fashion. Following this second tapping of his veins, the old man may have fainted for a time. His weariness had grown steadily more insupportable; for him a bed of nails would have been as easy to rest on as that cart.

From its wide summer arc the June sun lanced at the great city, striking through a worn blanket of clouds not yet changed from the night before. Pain in the head, and growing weariness, and—becoming gradually distinct from these—a most disquieting sense of something *wrong*. Intrinsically wrong with his existence, in the sense of something missing or crippled. As if an arm or leg were paralyzed, though that was not the case. He suffered a lack of powers that should have been his to call upon; and this lack was linked somehow with his want of a true name.

Periods of insensibility pocked all the old man's daylight hours that day, and a relatively full awareness returned to him only with the dawn of night.

As the day died, the first fact to impress itself upon his returning consciousness was that of Sally's presence in the room again. It was not yet quite dark, and she kept the blotched side of her face averted as she stood by his bed. Her shaking hands were extended towards the old man's shackled right wrist, and in her fingers was a key.

"Thank God yer awyke!" Her whisper was as tremulous as her fingers. "I found out they mean to . . . Can you walk?"

"I can."

"I 'opes to God you can. Now I knows yer a gentleman. Pledge now, by your honor, that when yer free you'll give me wot 'elp you can, in turn."

The old man quickly raised his head. "I pledge by all I hold most sacred, that I will help you and defend you afterward, if you can aid me now."

Her hand was on the steel, and yet she hesitated. "By helpin', I means you not goin' ter no perlice. I'll blindfold you an' lead you out o' this, and then you just clear out and ferget about it. I never been party t' no murder, and I can't do it now. Not a gent like you, so sweet and brave, an' . . . an' lovely."

"I swear to you that the police shall hear no word of this from me." Hope pumped new power into his whispering voice, into the leanly cabled muscles of his confined limbs.

"You say nothin' t' *no one*." She hissed it like a deadly threat. "Or it'll be my life an' yours as well!"

"To no one, then. Now quick, girl, quick!"

As on the previous morning, he could hear them coming long before she did. They were still many rooms away. He tried to hurry her, then had to alter plan and interject a warning; she was still fumbling with the key at the first lock when their brisk feet were about to enter the adjoining room. She had barely time to replace the keys on the shelf, beside the broken mirror, when the door opened and Rough-voice and the woman entered, masked, to stand dumbfounded at the sight of Sally where they had no reason to expect her.

The girl managed six words of attempted alibi, and one piteous outcry, before the man's fist knocked her down.

Hoisted to her feet by his ham-hand on her upper arm, she drooled out blood with her apology. Which was something about: ". . . on'y gettin' the gent a drink."

The gent, whom no one was bothering to watch, shook his head judiciously. It sounded very lame.

"Wot I wants ter know, right quick Sal, is why yer in this bloody room at all?"

"Lookin' fer you, I was. That's all, I swear!" Sal went on to explain why she had supposedly been in a hurry to locate Rough-voice. Her arguments were too oblique and fragmentary for the old man to grasp them at the time, or to remember them at this late date. But Sal's inquisitors seemed disposed, however grudgingly, to believe them. Bound on his cart he gave a slight nod of approval. Still no one was watching him.

From the man Sally might have escaped with no worse than a burst lip and a fierce warning; but there was yet the female of the species with whom she must contend.

In a commanding voice, which excitement turned hard-breathing and even more Germanic, the older woman urged: "Ve must impress upon t' girl t' seriousness uff tis." She gestured imperiously. Rough-voice obediently seized Sal and wrestled her into the next room, presumably better equipped for making impressions of the kind the woman had in mind. After one initial spasm of resistance, the unhappy girl ceased to struggle.

Now, thought the old man, honoring his pledge to Sal, and tried to summon up the army of his powers. The prospect of escape had acted on him as a stimulant, and he had now recovered far enough to know that unusual powers existed for him. Yet only a host of bemused ghosts responded to his call. They were the shades of energies that once had been, and might sometime be again, if only this mortal exhaustion did not kill him first.

In the other room the older woman's voice spoke softly, warmly, and with a sudden girlish eagerness. There was a rustle as of clothing being shifted, and then Sally cried out with true fierce pain, much louder than before. "Ah no, I meant no harm! Please no, I'll not do it ever again . . ."

Once more the scream. Then some metal implement was tossed aside, and a slight body slid through a man's grasp and crumpled on the floor, whining and gasping with ongoing pain. At about this point the doctor arrived, brisk as usual and ready for a good day's work. He had a few words of conversation with his co-workers, and delivered a short homily to Sal. She was allowed, as soon as she could stand, to make her way unsteady but unhindered from the building.

The doctor, masked, gowned, and gloved as before, soon looked in and helped himself to another sample of the old man's blood, with difficulties no smaller than before. Whatever portion of the day his study of this sample occupied, the doctor was not back again till dark. Meanwhile the old man had spent most of the daylight hours in tranced oblivion.

This last time, the doctor came into the room unmasked. This first free look at that thin cold young face with its thick blond mustache the old man correctly interpreted as an ominous sign.

"A very interesting patient you would make, old fellow. Very interesting indeed. But far too untypical, I fear, for our present needs. I would like very much to study you, just to satisfy my curiosity, but there is no time for that just now. And unfortunately no way for me to put you on ice until later." The physician bent closer to examine closely the skin of the old man's chest, and then sighed lightly. "I can't even tell if you were bitten by the fleas; if not, that would be another thumping great peculiarity . . . and given the present state of your blood, I doubt you'll live long enough to pose a threat as an informer or a potential witness. But of course that can't be left to chance. Dispose of him, Matthews."

"Arr, ra-ther. Now that 'e knows me name." Matthews (or Rough-voice), who had just come in, sounded quietly outraged.

"And my own face, as you observe. So do a thorough job. As I have every confidence you will."

Matthews shook his head. "I will need a bit o' help wi' the boat, is all. I think I'd best use the same way as before."

"Are none of the lads available?"

"Not right on hand, Guv. It's been a busy time."

"I can help." The woman had just come in, and was now taking off her mask. Her eyes, with the rest of the face now visible to set them off, looked harder than ever.

The doctor, brightening, turned to her. "It *would* certainly help, Frau Grafenstein, if you do not mind.

45

My own duties will prevent my leaving the building for some time."

"Mind a bit of exercise in a boat? Pah, of course not." The roses put into her cheeks by the brief work-out with Sally had not yet entirely faded. "I am not one uff your fragile ladies, doctor."

And it was the woman who first approached the cart. From some shelf on its lower half she brought up a pillow, with the idea of making the patient more comfortable. She pressed it firmly down upon the face of the supine old man, blocking both nose and mouth.

How easy for him to make his chest surge up and down a little, and then hold it quite still. To strain and quiver in all his limbs, and then let them relax.

Time passed.

"That's got 'im." Rough-voice gave his professional opinion flatly. Deferring to these specialists, the physician had already walked away, hurrying back to his own mysterious and demanding job.

The woman lifted the pillow, revealing the old man's face, his color ghastly (it had not been good to begin with), his mouth ajar and eyelids likewise. It was a corpse-like face that looked as if it might be stiffening already. He had seen death by suffocation often enough to be able to mime it without difficulty. What had he not seen, indeed? Well, much. An animal like that still snuffling in the room beyond, to name one thing.

The steel fetters continued to hold his arms and legs, but were now somehow disconnected from his cart.

"These irons'll myke just a good bit o' weight if we leaves 'em on."

The woman answered: "Yes, that's all right, we have more. And leave his gown on him. We should have to dispose of that in any case."

The old man's whole body and its fetters were slid into what felt like an oilcloth bag, of a size and shape to hold a body handily. Then he was lifted free of the bed and draped over Matthews' broad shoulder. In this way he was carried out of the room of his imprisonment and through another room, then down a long flight of stairs, the bearer grunting out a pithy comment or two about the unexpected weight. Frau Grafenstein marched briskly on ahead, to open doors.

At last they came to outdoor air, enriched with horse-smells, starched with coal-smoke, larded with the stale cosmopolitan essence of the Thames. The smells of night and of damp earth served as effective stimuli for memory, or should have done.

Obviously they intended to sink him in the river, and that would be that, no? Well, no, he thought, for he had already survived smothering. Actually he was far from helpless. The thing he had to do . . . he should be able to . . .

Energized by the approach of midnight, the battered brain within the aged skull fought to repair its broken weapons. To remember the things that must and could be done would be much easier if he were able to recall just who and what he *was* . . . .

He was borne on the strong man's shoulder down a ladder, with river-smell strong and sounds of water lapping near, and then he was cast roughly into the bottom of what must have been a rather large rowboat. It swayed only a little with the weight of the three people boarding, rubbing its sides against pilings to the starboard and port. The need for the lady's aid was soon apparent: two pairs of hands, one working at the bow and one at the stern, were required to work the heavy craft out of what must have been a place of snug concealment beneath a dock, a berth into which it was kept wedged by the river's current.

As soon as the craft was drifting free, Frau G. sat down in the stern and rested, one booted foot comfortably propped upon the old man's unmoving hip, whilst Matthews broke out a pair of oars.

A dozen or so strokes, and the man began complaining yet again. He was having an unexpectedly tough time transporting this particular cargo over running water. Ah, folk would grumble less if they knew more. He might have had a far more difficult evening than he did.

"Ach, man," Frau Grafenstein admonished briskly, "put your back into it." The old man in his bag could almost picture her shaking a stern finger. "Neither uff your passengers iss very big or heavy. And you ought to be used to this particular trip by now."

"That old un's heavier than you might think, Missus," Matthews grunted, pulling hard as bidden. "Somethin' queer about him. In general, I means. Weren't there?" Grunt again. "Bit o' rough current tonight, it feels like."

"One uff these nights you may be rowing this way, with your young cousin, done up zo." She treated the old man to a familiar joggle from her boot.

"Nar. With all respeck, Missus, I 'spect Sal will be a good 'un now. You made a bit of an impression on 'er tonight."

"I trust that you are right." The woman sighed; it was a delicate and almost feminine sound. Then in a little while she said: "This should be far enough. Those new electric lights across the river will be too close for comfort if we go on."

"Ar."

The oars stopped and were shipped inboard. Again two strong hands grappled the old man's oilcloth bag. They put him straight over the gunwale, wrappings, and weighty bonds and all, without delay or ceremony, almost without a splash.

Cold water tried to fasten teeth into his skin, but he was callous to its bite. His breathless lips were pressed fastidiously tight against the dirty tide. The muted shock of immersion served as a needed tonic for his brain. His powers armed themselves, were ghosts no longer, although still lacking intellectual control. He felt his iron manacles drop off, and with them the shrouding bag. But it was not the metal that melted or the cloth that tore. Some other object lost its solidity, rose like a spectral bubble through the water, and then slowly regained its substance and its shape. Now the old man stood dripping on the pier, still clad in his hospital victim's gown. His burgeoning powers were ringed around him now, a bodyguard invisible and awesome, though in disordered ranks. Still missing was their captain, the last great power: his true name.

The boat had rowed up to the far end of the pier, where it was letting off the woman now. Looking between piles of shipping crates, the old man could see her quite easily, despite the forty yards or so of smoggy night between.

"Stuff and nonsense." Her voice was plain, not loud but brisk. "Uff course I shall be all right." And then her military walk came spattering the last rain's shallow mirrors in his direction, shivering the stray gleams of electric lights ranked somewhere on the Thames' far bank. Matthews meanwhile had stayed in the boat, and was now rowing it out toward midstream, inadvertently putting between himself and the old man such a stretch of running water that the latter in his weakened state perceived it as an effective barrier.

The woman's jaunty footfalls came on toward him through the night, behind tall piles of crates. All that old man needed to do was stand there in the shadow of a disused boatshed, waiting.

She came in sight again, now close enough for her to see him also. He waited almost storklike on his long bare legs below that ridiculous shirt in which she had helped to dress him. His face that she had pillowed only minutes earlier was in the shadow now, but still she could scarcely have mistaken his figure in her path for that of any other man. Her stride faltered, and the hard dominance of her own face cracked like a clay mask.

But . . . not one of your fragile ladies, as she had herself remarked. She could not avoid him, and after faltering once she marched on, pulling out a pistol. It barked like a toy dog from its abbreviated barrel, and sharp pain, ineffectual metallic pain, lanced the old man through the chest and flew on past him, even as his long arms reached out . . . .

At last his combined hunger and thirst were satisfied—he had not known how strong the craving was till he began to gratify it—and he lifted his head, licking a lip thoughtfully, looking and listening. The pier he stood on, and its adjoining piers, were quite deserted. Somewhere down the long water-corridor of shipping that twisted toward the sea, foghorns were beginning conversation.

He held the body out at arm's length. Hard boots and limp hands hung straight toward their ruffled images in muddy, moving water. In that mirror the woman's body was suspended completely without support, its draperies of clothing tucked up by invisible force-at knees and shoulders.

It pleased him to bestow, in his own mind, an epitaph: *Not one of your fragile ladies*. With that he let the drained thing splash.

In the brief struggle the hospital gown has been torn almost completely loose, and now with complete unconcern for either modesty or warmth he lets it fall. He sees the body drift and sink, and float again, but already his thoughts are elsewhere.

That he will now turn upon his remaining persecutors and endeavor to hunt them down is beyond question. But should he, can he, begin that necessary task before he has his own identity in hand?

With food his strength is waxing, but he is still in mortal need of rest, and still he cannot remember. Why has he known no fear, through all these perils? He is not immortal, no, far from it, but . . .

Why does the water not give him his reflection back? And, how came he flowing like fog out of the water, neither the tide nor steel bonds able to hold him? Why had that heavy, leaden bullet done no worse than kiss him with a sharp sting as it passed through his body?

There are a hundred questions more.

One above all: *Who is he?*

IV

Following Miss Sarah Tarlton's first visit to Baker Street, Sherlock Holmes spent the remainder of the day in concluding his work upon one or two routine matters that he had been investigating at the request of the police. On the following morning he went out alone, quite early, and was gone for several hours.

"I have just set in motion several inquiries concern--ing the mysterious Dr. John Scott," he said upon returning. "If you are free after lunch, Watson, I hope you will accompany me to the warehouse where he was supposedly identified. Your medical knowledge may well prove useful in any discussion of the equipment that was removed."

I of course agreed, and before two o'clock we were in a cab, on our way to the London Docks at Shadwell. The warehouse was one of a number of long, low, shed-like buildings set close by the waterfront. After passing the desks of several clerks, we were admitted to the office of the superintendent.

Superintendent Marlowe was a man of sixty or thereabouts, powerfully built and energetic in appearance. It was his habit to rise, at the least pretext, from behind his desk, as if the confinement of the small space there were too much for his nature to bear.

He pressed our hands in greeting, as if we had come at his own invitation. "Very pleased to meet you, Dr. Watson. Mr. Holmes, this is a real honor. I suppose it's this business of the medical materials that you've come about? Yes, as I thought. Well, you may be sure we don't release goods to people who have no right to take them."

"I am reassured to hear it, Superintendent," Holmes responded. "How did you come to guess the nature of our business?"

"Well, sir, when young Miss Tarlton was here, with the gentleman who was helping her, she spoke of an investigation. With which, says I, I shall be only too glad to comply, provided that it be conducted legally and in good form. And for which I am now ready, having the papers in question right here." Unlocking a drawer in his desk, the superintendent brought out a sheaf of documents. "Take my word for it, gentlemen, these are all in good order."

"May I?" My companion eagerly reached out a long arm. In his other hand, Holmes held two of the letters written by John Scott to his fiancee, and now he brought all together to the window, the better to compare handwriting. When in a few moments he turned back to face us, his appearance was somewhat crestfallen. "Mr. Marlowe, I advise you to keep these papers in a secure place. With regard to your claim to have accurately identified John Scott, they will be of enormous importance should this matter ever come to the courts."

"Ha! The courts, is it? Indeed, I'll keep 'em safe." And Marlowe hastily accepted the papers back.

"Another question or two, if you would, Superintendent, before we go."

"Of course."

"Did any of the men who came for the equipment—I am assuming there were several, even if some were only carters—did any of them say anything about the purpose for which the items were wanted, or where they were being taken?"

"Yes, Dr. Scott had carters with him, and a pair of wagons." Marlowe, who had just sat down again behind his desk, got up, to stand as if lost in thought. "Wait a bit. I did ask if the things were going to be wanted in London; if so, it might have been easiest and best for him to let 'em stop right here for a time. But 'No,' says he, 'I mean to put them on a goods train for Portsmouth. The ship I want next is sailing from there.' And so I thought no more about it."

"Indeed." Holmes looked at the superintendent keenly. "Those were his exact words?"

"Yes, I'll testify to that. I pride myself that I've a fine memory for where things are kept, and whose they are, and also for who says what."

"I am glad to hear it. Did you by any chance mention to Dr. Scott that his friend Peter Moore had been here only a day earlier?"

"Why, yes sir, of course I did; but the doctor just gave me a quick look, as much as to say it was none of my particular business. The way he looked just made me think that there was perhaps some rivalry or trouble between the two of them."

"I see. But did Mr. Peter Moore give you the same impression?"

"Why, no sir. I had the idea from him that the other was his particular friend, and they should be very glad to see each other again."

Our visit was soon finished. When Holmes and I

were once more outside the warehouse, I asked: "Then the papers showed conclusively that the man who signed and paid for the equipment was indeed John Scott?"

"Let us walk a little, Watson, before we try to hail a cab. How bracing the atmosphere of the docks can sometimes be—the sense of the great world impinging upon us with all its mysteries and complications. No, I am afraid that the signatures show that the man who wrote them was an imposter—though he must have put in a good deal of time and effort in practicing from a true copy. I have no doubt that any first-rate handwriting expert will be able to convince a jury of the forgery. But let the superintendent and his staff believe that those documents justify them, and you may depend upon it that the signatures will be secure until we need them. Also, a real American would have said 'freight train' and not 'goods train'—unless he were consciously practicing to speak like an Englishman. It is an additional point, though hardly in itself conclusive.

"Meanwhile, Watson, the question to which we must address ourselves is—why?"

"You mean, why should a man have posed as Dr. Scott to steal the things? Their value must be considerable."

"Considerable, but hardly vast. Remember that the impostor paid, without a murmur, several hundred pounds to get them. Now, there are surely only a few places where a thief could hope to sell such specialized equipment. Honest researchers would hesitate to buy it from him. So why on earth should a clever rogue, or a gang of them, go to such trouble and expense for loot which one might think would do them little good?"

"It does seem odd, put in that way."

"There is another question, Watson, by no means unrelated—how were they able to obtain or forge good identification papers for Dr. Scott? . . . but halloa! Is that not the figure of our old friend Lestrade I see?"

We happened to be crossing a short street which ended right at dockside, thirty or forty yards away. Standing on a pier near the street's end was a short, wiry man in a gray coat. Two uniformed policemen stood talking with this individual, or rather listening to him. He waved his arms, and made emphatic nodding motions with his head to give force to his words, which at our distance were inaudible.

By silent agreement, Holmes and I at once turned in that direction, and presently we had stepped onto the pier. There was a tension visible in Lestrade, as we drew near him, that I had seldom seen before. His sallow face was pinched and worried when he dismissed the constables and turned toward us, but his expression changed wonderfully as soon as he caught sight of Sherlock Holmes.

"Mr. Holmes . . . Dr. Watson . . . I'm blessed if there's anyone in the world I'd rather set eyes on at this moment. In fact, Mr. Holmes, I sent a man to Baker Street an hour ago to try to fetch you."

Holmes nodded. "No doubt there is a murder at hand which presents some features of uncommon interest? Where is the body?"

Lestrade lowered his voice. "It's not thirty yards behind me, lying right on this pier. And this is the worst one I've seen since the days of Jack the Ripper. Thank heaven there's a clue or two . . ." Lestrade paused, frowning at Holmes. "Here now! I hadn't said a word about its being murder."

"Tut! When I see one of the leading detectives of

Scotland Yard so obviously worried, I know that he is baffled, if only temporarily, by some mystery of the first importance. And the Thames is surely the great traditional repository for the central piece of evidence in crimes of blood." And Sherlock Holmes briskly rubbed his hands, as if he stood before a fire and the day were chill. Far back in his gray eyes, a spark of something keen and lively had been born.

The three of us were now out of earshot of all possible eavesdroppers. Even the two uniformed men had moved away, evidently going on Lestrade's orders to keep the pier and the street nearby clear of curious onlookers; some idlers had in fact gathered a short distance up the street and were gazing in our direction. But despite our isolation, Lestrade turned his head to right and left before he spoke, and his voice now was lower still.

"Murder's almost too mild a word for it, gentlemen. The throat was torn right away, as if by—well, claws or teeth. Not like the Ripper's handiwork, really. More as if a real beast might have done it."

"Then perhaps," I suggested, "it might have been in fact an animal?"

"A big, savage dog, for instance, Dr. Watson? Maybe. Wait'll you see. More likely a tiger, if you can find one running loose in London. But then an animal would not have thrown her body into the river afterwards, hey? Or rifled her purse. And then there's the gun."

Holmes, almost twinkling, put out a hand. "Slowly, Lestrade. Will you show us the body? And, while we are on our way, you might tell us how it came to be discovered."

"Right." Lestrade drew a deep breath. "This way

then, gentlemen." He began to lead us out along the pier, most of which was occupied by stacks of what appeared to be abandoned crates, so that we were soon hidden from any casual observers on the shore. "Mind your step here; these planks are almost rotted through in places. The body was seen floating in the water a little before noon today, by two dock-laborers about to sit down in what they thought would be a quiet spot, to eat their lunch. These men are both of good character, as far as we have been able to make out, and there is nothing to connect them with the crime."

I now could see another police helmet ahead, above another pile of crates. Lestrade, who was beginning to look haggard again, continued: "And this's no woman of the streets, gentlemen. Another difference to prove the Ripper's not back on the job after a nine-year rest. Not that it'll matter to the papers. I'm mortally certain they're going to scream Jack's struck again."

By this time we had rounded the last barrier, and had come in full sight of the uniformed officer who impassively stood guard, and of that which he guarded. A still form lay on the planks, covered with a gray blanket of a type I recognized as being commonly used by the medical examiner's office.

Lestrade bent and drew the blanket back. The woman lay on her back, fully clothed, her sodden garments being disarranged only in the region of the throat. There, as the inspector had said, the flesh was lacerated with extreme savagery, as if the victim had indeed fallen before the fangs or talons of some monstrous beast. Her arms were outflung, her exposed face and hands as pallid as marble. Her hair, still stringy as if from complete immersion, was dark, streaked with gray, and I should have put her age as somewhere between forty and fifty.

Holmes, his keen eyes avidly grasping every detail, bent low over the body like a hound taking the scent. "The boots, Lestrade, appear to be of German make."

"I shouldn't be surprised, Mr. Holmes. She's a German subject, and her name's Wilhelmina Grafenstein—or that was the name and identity she used lodging at the Great Eastern Hotel. Some stationery in her purse—I'll show you in a minute—put us onto that, and we've already had one of the room clerks over to identify her. No word of any next of kin as yet. I've been holding back on having the body removed, hoping you might be available for consultation."

Holmes hardly appeared to be listening. "I take it this is the exact spot where she was first laid down, directly on being brought out of the water? To be sure. And where, precisely, was the body floating when the two workmen first saw it?"

Leaning out a little over the water, Lestrade pointed straight down past our feet, indicating the pier's support of close-set wooden pilings.

Holmes glanced upstream and back again. "Exactly where one might expect a body to lodge, if it had been thrown in carelessly from the next pier."

The inspector drew himself up a little. "That was my own thought, Mr. Holmes. I've been over there and looked about, of course, and found an interesting clue or two."

Beyond some twenty or thirty yards of dirty water, another uniformed man was partially visible as he stood on the next pier beside a shabby boatshed. This policeman greeted us with a small salute, when we had reached him by a roundabout walk along the cluttered dockside. Besides the small boathouse on this pier, there stood some cargo-handling machinery in dilapidated condition, and again some weathered crates and bales.

Where Lestrade had placed his sentry, about halfway out along the pier, three things having no connection with the business of shipping and storage lay on the worn boards. These objects were two or three yards apart from each other, and around each a circle had been drawn in yellow chalk, no doubt by Lestrade's own hand.

The supposed clue nearest the water's edge was a crumpled piece of wet, gray cloth. One extended sleeve showed that this was a garment of some kind, but I could tell nothing more from looking at its shapeless heap. The second object was a woman's handbag, open, looking new and undoubtedly expensive. And the third, a trifle farther than the others from the pier's edge, was a small pistol.

"These things are all exactly as I found them, Mr. Holmes. Except for looking into the handbag, as I've explained, I haven't touched a thing. I don't know as this shirt or whatever it is has any connection with the crime at all, but still . . ."

Holmes' only answer was a distracted grunt. He was already in action. At first ignoring the items in the chalked circles, he devoted himself to a methodical inspection of the whole area. At times he bent until his eye was almost in contact with the planks; again, he stood at his full height to examine carefully the rusted metal of the fixed machinery, and the peeling sides of the boathouse.

Here he suddenly gave a small, sharp cry of triumph,

pulled out a pocketknife, and with controlled energy dug into the faded wood at a point a little above eye level. In a minute or two he had extracted a small object, which he held out on his palm for our inspection. It was a bullet, much flattened by the resistance of the stout wooden beam by which its flight had been arrested.

Before Lestrade or I could offer much in the way of comment upon this discovery, Holmes was off again. For several minutes he squatted beside the boathouse, frowning at some peculiar scratches that I now perceived upon the deck planks there. These suggested to me that the wood had been raked with sharp metal tines, like those of a pitchfork, or perhaps by the claws of some large, strong animal. Holmes measured them carefully with his pocket tape, but said nothing about them at the time.

Only when he had completed this general survey did Holmes turn to what Lestrade had termed the clues. Of these, the weapon was the first my friend picked up.

Lestrade said quickly: "Of the Derringer type, as you'll note, Mr. Holmes. A two-shot model, and it smells as if at least one's been fired."

"That is so." Holmes had opened the breech, closed it again, and was now scrutinizing the pistol keenly through a small lens he had whipped out of his pocket. "And I observe on it many small scratches, almost randomly distributed; this gun has been carried loose in a handbag or purse, rather than a holster or a man's pocket, for some considerable period of time." Handing the gun over to Lestrade, Holmes moved to pick up the purse.

"I did look into that pretty thoroughly, Mr. Holmes," said the official detective in a somewhat defensive tone. "There's precious little in it that's going to be of any help to us, beyond what I've already found. You'll note that there's no money left to speak of."

Holmes pulled from the purse some sheets of the writing-paper that Lestrade had mentioned earlier. All were blank save for the Great Eastern letterhead. Crouching, Holmes set these down on the damp planking, then pulled out the rest of the purse's contents. On the paper he placed a small bunch of keys, of which I could see that some were for common locks and some for Chubb's. After the keys there came some stamps, a few pence and a shilling, and a small handkerchief. That was all.

Tossing Lestrade the empty purse, Holmes muttered something impatiently, and moved on to pick up and smooth out the crumpled garment. It proved to be a peculiar-looking sort of shirt or gown, which was very damp, and left a wet mark where it had lain upon the lighter dampness of the wood. Holmes with his long fingers held it up by the shoulders, as if intending to measure it against his own spare frame. We all three of us gazed at the garment—my two companions looking rather blankly at it, if I may say so—for some time.

"I have seen a similar shirt," I ventured to remark, at length, "used in an institution for the criminally insane. Its design allows changing the dress of very violent patients, without undoing the strong restraints that have been placed upon their limbs. Observe how the sleeves are divided lengthwise, and their sections held together with small cloth ties. This allows the shirt to be put on and taken off while the patient's wrists remain fettered."

"Precisely," said Holmes in a dry voice. It was his

customary way of acknowledging the receipt of some useful bit of information. He turned the shirt round in his hands and sniffed at it.

"Well, gentlemen, we seem to have the identity of our killer all but settled now." Lestrade took off his hat, ran a hand through his dark hair, and settled the hat on firmly once again. "It's a real maniac we're after—the nature of the wound alone shows that. This shirt shows that he's just escaped from somewhere, and once we learn where, we'll have a name and a description, and we'll also be in a fair way to know where he's likely to turn up next. Run to a pattern, these lunatics do, as you're no doubt aware, Doctor."

Summoning the constable who had been standing guard, Lestrade issued urgent orders; the man turned and trotted off along the pier toward the shore. The inspector turned back to us. "They'll have the message at the Yard in a few minutes, and inquiries will be going out by wire at once. Well, Mr. Holmes, it begins to look after all as if there was no need to trouble you with this case . . . hallo, what is it now?"

Holmes was staring fixedly at the garment which he still held in his hands. I, at his side, saw with some uneasiness that a tinge of pallor had come into his face, and there raced through my mind an apprehension lest his nervous symptoms of the previous March be recurring. Following his gaze, I discovered its object at the same time as Lestrade, who had now moved closer.

"Ah," commented the inspector, in a voice devoid of understanding. "Holes. One in the front and one in back."

"Indubitably." Holmes was nettled by this slow-wittedness, and the color returned fully to his cheeks. "They are holes. And what do you make of them?"

"Well. I don't know as I'm prepared to say."

"Oh, out with it, man. They're bullet-holes, of course, or I'm prepared to change my career to basket-weaving. Watson, which side of this garment would ordinarily be worn in front? As I thought. It is the front-side bullet-hole, then, that is so well marked with powder burns, showing that the shot was fired at extreme close range. While the hole in back is marked with—nothing. Nothing, mark you, neither burns nor blood."

Holmes' voice had fallen off, as if he now spoke only to himself. Falling into a moment of reverie, he stared off across the river as if the hazed wharves there on the south bank might possess some secret information. Then with a shake of his head he roused himself. "Upon my word, Watson, business is looking up. A month of routine, and then two intriguing puzzles in as many days."

Turning back to Lestrade, Holmes asked: "There is, I suppose, no bullet wound upon the woman's body?"

"The medical examiner and I both looked, sir. There is none."

"Then let her poor clay be removed." Holmes gestured toward the other pier. "Take her up tenderly, as I believe the poet has it." But he was actually smiling as he spoke. At the moment the woman's tragedy meant less to him than the intellectual challenge it represented.

Once more he held the garment up. "I think you must agree, Watson, that if this was on the body of a man when these holes were made, the bullet must have passed through or very near his vital organs."

"Yes, certainly."

Holmes was now examining the small holes closely

64

with his lens. "The condition of these edges indicates that the bullet passed through the garment after it was wetted. It is still far from dry; let us say that it was wetted no more than about twelve hours ago—probably by immersion, for last night there was no heavy rain. All these facts are consistent with the hypothesis that the holes were made about the same time that the woman was killed, and the one shot fired from her pistol, the bullet lodging in the shed wall."

"Well, it may be. But I don't see, Mr. Holmes, how all this theorizing now is likely to help us catch a maniac."

Holmes let his hand holding the garment fall to his side. His voice was distant. "Lestrade, let me call your attention also to the singular matter of the blood."

Lestrade and I both gazed around. "I see no blood," the Scotland Yard man complained.

"That, of course, is the singular matter. There is not much left of the German lady's throat except one gaping wound, which must have bled her life away in moments. But on the boards of this pier there are visible only four small drops of blood—"

"I saw none at all," Lestrade protested.

"—four small drops. And none at all upon her clothing, where some stain would seem inevitable, even after immersion in the river."

I ventured: "Is it possible that that terrible wound might have been inflicted while the woman was in the water?"

"Bravo, Watson! But then, why four drops, instead of none at all? And the absence of the woman's blood is not the only puzzle. One would think that the man who wore this shirt must have bled copiously himself if he were alive when shot. Even if he were already dead, the bullet's passage should have left some traces, at least, of flesh and blood upon the fabric. Nor do I see here threads from an undergarment, that might have completely absorbed a small amount of such debris.''

"Well, I cannot fathom it," Lestrade admitted. ''But the woman is certainly dead, and I do not believe that these details are likely to prove of much importance.''

"Holmes," I suggested, "is it possible that this odd garment was draped on some clothier's dummy or mannikin when it was fired at? Or simply held up empty, and the bullet-hole made, with the intention of leaving a totally false clue for the police?''

My friend shook his head. "It will not do. Would the killer, having put himself to such trouble, then throw into the river the main evidence of his crime, a corpse that might easily have drifted out to sea without ever being discovered? And for whose benefit was the false clue made? For the police? It is only chance that they noticed the rag at all. Was it done to lead me astray? But it is only by chance, again, that I was called in on the investigation. No, Watson. Besides, the indications are that a real man has recently worn this shirt.''

"Indications?" I asked.

"Well, the bloodstains, for example.''

"Here, now!" Lestrade was beginning to bristle. "You've just now told us that the bullet drew no blood.''

My friend spread out the shirt again in his long fingers—which, I saw unhappily, had just acquired a slight tremor. "That is so. But I shall be very much surprised if these traces here upon the right sleeve, just at the elbow, do not prove to be dried blood. The spots are quite small but they are several in number, as if more than one sample of blood had been drawn from the wearer. Yes, Lestrade, a man has worn this garment recently. But apart from the obvious facts that he is tall, lean, robust though no longer young, and is or was an unwilling patient, there is as yet little that I can say about him." He crumpled the shirt together in his hands, but continued to stare at it.

Lestrade opened his mouth, closed it again, then spoke at last. "I won't argue any of those points with you, Mr. Holmes." Still, he appeared to be not at all convinced.

Holmes raised his head and smiled, like one recalled from an unpleasant train of thought. "Surely 'obvious' is not too strong a word. Assuming this garment to have fit its wearer at all, its length indicates that his height must be at least roughly equal to my own. This is borne out by the length of the sleeves, which were worn fully extended, not rolled or turned back; although the cloth ties at the back of the shirt have been ripped loose, those upon the sleeves are still fastened, down to the last strings at the wrists." He paused. "Also, the bullet's passage was a rising one from front to back, which of course suggests a gun in the hand of a short person firing at a tall one. That would be perfectly consistent with the high lodging-place of the bullet in the shed wall."

I was mystified. "Holmes, I thought you had just proven that this garment could not have been on a man when the bullet passed through it."

My friend did not answer. Still gazing at the offending shirt, he shook it as if a drop of truth might be squeezed out of it like water.

Since Holmes' slighting remarks about the discovery of clues being a matter of chance with the police,

Lestrade had been scowling. Now he shook his head. "It seems to me that the evidence here—the hard, solid evidence, that is—is pretty plain and straightforward. As to the height of the man who wore this shirt, I fancy we'll know that soon enough when we find out where he's escaped from. Oh, I'll grant you he's likely tall, but as to the rest of your guesses, sir, I have my doubts."

"Guesses?" Holmes' temper flared for a moment, so sharply that both Lestrade and I were taken somewhat by surprise. But only a moment, and then my friend was calm again. I could see it was not really Lestrade's attitude which had upset him; that was only an additional irritation coming on top of something that had struck him far more deeply.

Holmes went on: "That the wearer is, or was, lean is perhaps a riskier deduction than his height. But the close tying of the sleeves assures us that at least his arms are far from being grossly fat. And something of his age can be deduced from this short gray hair, evidently from a hirsute arm, caught in one of the small knots.

"He is, or was, a patient of some kind, as evidenced by the fact that his blood was sampled. As for his being robust and unwilling, surely the usual elderly inmate of an asylum or hospital would be clothed in something more ordinary. Anyone wearing this special garment may be presumed to be under strong restraint. Nor, perhaps, is the common variety of ill old man likely to be drenched in carbolic acid, and then to have a bullet fired through his nightshirt as he enjoys his customary midnight stroll along the docks."

"Well, of course—all that is rather plain and straightforward, as I say."

"Quite so." Holmes smiled, and for the moment seemed completely himself. "Nevertheless, I believe I shall just keep this garment—that is, if the official police have no objection?"

"Keep it, and welcome." The Scotland Yard man, too, had regained his good humor. "When we've heard just which madman has jumped a fence, and have got our hands on him, maybe there'll be a good explanation for that strange bullet hole—if anyone's still interested."

"Perhaps." Holmes rolled up the shirt and stuffed it into his coat pocket. "Come along then, Watson—I feel the need to give my violin a bit of exercise. Meanwhile, Lestrade, if you were to ask my advice as to your own best course of action, beyond inquiring for escaped madmen—"

"I do indeed, Mr. Holmes. You've steered me right before this."

"—it is to have the bottom of the river dragged, in the area near these two piers."

The other seemed a trifle disappointed. "And just what, Mr. Holmes, are we to go a-looking in the river for?"

Holmes spoke thoughtfully. "I should look, Lestrade, if I were you, for any—grotesque—oddity."

"Oddity?" Lestrade plainly did not understand; no more did I, I must confess.

"You may find none. But when there are several, as I find here, experience suggests that one more is not unlikely."

V

Well fed there in the dead of night, the old man—no, let me be done with this transparent literary coyness, this pretense that that old man was someone else. Well fed, I say, I found myself greatly restored in strength, although each atom of my being still cried out for the repose that my days of prisoned immobility had not afforded me.

Rummaging in the woman's purse, I took what money came to hand, considering it my due as the spoils of a just war. As I recall, there were some eight or nine pounds in gold sovereigns, silver crowns, and shillings, as well as a five pound Bank of England note. This last served me to wrap the coins for carrying, I being at the moment pocketless. Then, so overwhelming was my need for rest, that naked as I was I lay down like a wounded animal, seeking the darkest shadows close beside the abandoned boathouse.

The plain wood should not have been too hard for an old soldier, but it might as well have been bare thorns and jagged glass for all the rest it could provide me. Even exerting all my powers of will, which are not inconsiderable, I could not force my muscles to relax. When I tried, my body tossed this way and that, a puppet on a madman's strings. First one set of muscles and then another tensed. My left hand held my money in a spasmodic clutch, whilst my right clawed uncontrollably at the rough planks. In a few minutes I gave up and got to my feet again, though my knees quivered with my weariness, thinking that if my energy must be spent it had better be to some good purpose.

So I began to walk. With no clear idea of where I was within London, still less of where I might be going, I let my feet carry me away from the docks, along one narrow, deserted way after another, keeping always to the shadows. Somewhere, I knew, there existed a place, a condition, wherein I could rest . . . some haven must exist for me, else I never could have lived at all. But still my battered memory would not produce the vital information.

Meanwhile I had a secondary need, and toward its satisfaction I could try to make a conscious plan. I looked for a chance to obtain clothing as I prowled on, my money still clutched in my hand.

Although the time was now past midnight—about the time I left the docks, I heard church clocks tolling twelve—not all the streets of the East End were yet asleep. Throngs of the poor working folk, the unemployed, the beggars, thieves, and prostitutes still walked the pavements of these lighted thoroughfares, and many of their shop doors were still open. Laughter drifted to my ears, and music, ground out on a handorgan by a street entertainer.

I paused, in a gloomy vantage point, to watch. Past the mouth of my dark mews there rumbled wagons, whose horses pricked their ears in my direction but then turned away their heads in silence, keeping a secret from their masters. The smells of gin and beer, tobacco and cheap perfume came mingling softly with the night's new fog. I was standing, although I did not know it at the time, in Shadwell, not far from the noisome slums of Whitechapel. It was not a part of London that would have been familiar to me even had I been in full possession of my faculties.

Farther toward the gaslit regions I could not venture naked, and so turned back to midnight territory. Here the night was not entirely silent either. And the way was far from uninhabited, though it looked empty at first glance. When I focused my keen senses and my keener purpose, I could detect in almost every quarter wheezy breathing and the movement, in uneasy sleep, of ragged limbs. These came from almost any spot that offered some concealment and the promise of a little shelter against rain and wind—a doorway here, a row of dustbins there, a hedge across the way.

Although in December the situation might have been quite different, on such a balmy night in early June there were great throngs of London vagabonds, of both sexes and all ages, who preferred the risks of freedom to the gray walls of workhouse or charitable shelter. With an effortless stealth that kept my own presence unseen and unheard, I slid from one secreted sleeper to the next, inspecting them and passing on. Only a cat upon a windowsill reacted to my soft passage, with a faint snarl of vague concern. She quieted when I had looked into her yellow eyes.

So many derelicts were abroad hereabouts that it took me only a few minutes to locate a sleeping man whose physical measurements quite closely approximated my own. He was a-shudder already with some nightmare, his long limbs trembling, as I reached inside the angle of the disused doorway where he slept, and hauled him to his feet, with such a good grip on his collar that the seams of the ragged coat I coveted at once began to yield.

"Softly!" The word hissed from my lips in low but fierce command. I had seen that my client's mouth was opening, even before his eyelids began to flutter, and his larynx was in a preparatory state of vibration, tuning up for a mad scream of terror.

"Softly!" I urged him. "And those dreams of wealth that you must sometimes nurse shall find at least modest fulfillment. But the first loud sound you utter must be drowned out at once by the sharp crackling of your own bones—and *that* is such a revolting noise that I grow angry if I am forced to listen to it. Surely you will not choose to anger me?"

Whilst I was reasoning with him thus, his eyes opened in the worn leather of his face—they seemed to go on opening forever—and fixed on me. The few bad teeth remaining in his mouth were like to break themselves with chattering. And his trembling legs, their joints at every moment seeking a new angle, seemed utterly unable to support his meager weight. But fortunately—for both of us, perhaps—the scream still hung unvoiced within his throat.

Having made sure of this, I eased my grip a trifle, to let his own feet assume most of their rightful load. "I mean you no harm, my man," I went on. "I simply require your rags, or those of someone of your shape, and I see no reason why you should not be the one to benefit from my generosity. In payment for the abominable clothing you are wearing, I offer this." And between thumb and forefinger I held up a gold sovereign. "A fair price, is it not?"

It was of course a princely overpayment. Yet I was forced to repeat my offer several times before the oaf could master his terrors sufficiently to stammer out a crude agreement. So protracted was this delay, and the fumble-fingered unbuttoning which followed, that I came near letting him fall back to the pavement, and going on my way in search of someone brighter with whom to trade.

In glancing back over the account of this event I have just written, I am convinced that some of my modern readers will have doubts (to say the least) that I should have been so patient and generous when I so sorely needed clothing. Why did not I, with all my boasted stealth and night-vision, break into some house or shop and steal garments that were clean and whole? Or waylay some victim in the dark and strip him forcibly? Well, I shall return to this point later. For the present, let me only remark that I cannot, and never could, abide a thief.

Thus I concluded purchase of cap, coat, shirt, trousers, and a pair of shoes that would never have come close to fitting me had the soles still been in reasonable communion with the uppers. These clothes were aswarm in their every decayed seam with a variety of vermin, who at my silent shout of command leaped one and all, like sailors from a drowning ship, onto the cobblestones. This dominating rapport with less-than-human life was as much part of me as my pulse, and in my addled state I never remarked to myself upon the fact that the folk around me gave no evidence of enjoying any such power.

With my nakedness now covered, I could walk openly along the lighted streets. In that quarter of the city there walked many who had no better garb than mine. The late shops all seemed to be closing now, but I thought that in the morning I would be able to enter one and buy some better clothes . . . if I survived till then.

I was now grown so tired that only an effort of will kept me from staggering openly. In this way I moved on through the foggy streets, no conscious goal in mind. When *in extremis* it is not the intellect I trust, but something deeper and more elemental, whether it be called blind Fortune, or a warrior's instincts.

The city darkened as lights went out in one window after another. Brushing past me in the murk, the homeless and the relatively prosperous alike had turned their thoughts to shelter and to sleep. My own limbs now felt not much stronger than those of the man from whom I had my clothing. Only the fact that it was as yet not much past midnight gave me the strength I needed to move on. Every instinct warned me that from this hour my strength must wane, till dawn came like a fire to burn away my life—unless before dawn I had found rest.

By now my wanderings had brought me out upon the great thoroughfare called Commercial Road. Comparing what I saw about me with the blotched palimpsest of my memory, I gained some vague awareness of my location within London, and judged that Limehouse must be near ahead. Whether to push on farther to the east, or turn my steps some other way, I could not immediately decide. I stumbled and nearly fell, less from my broken shoes than from sheer deadly weariness. Folk hurried past in the slum street, paying no attention to my difficulties. Even my will wavered momentarily. Then I stoked up the flickering fires of life within my soul, and chose.

Scarcely had I proceeded fifty yards along the dim

street of my selection, when the flare of a private gaslight came into view immediately ahead, shining full upon a sign whose painted message I at once accepted as an omen. In bold lettering it promised to all in need the solace of their Savior, in the most eminently practical form of food and lodging.

Though there was money in my pockets, I had so far avoided all hotels and lodging houses, feeling certain in my bones that their soft beds would offer me no more repose than had my prisoner's cot, or the rough planking of the pier. But this hostel, with its tender of more than ordinary help, seemed something different, and I was immediately drawn to it.

I had, as I was later to realize, chanced upon one of the first shelters operated by the Salvation Army. The sturdy outer doors were on the verge of closing for the night, but their keeper—a charity case himself, to judge by his apparel—delayed long enough to admit me, along with one additional latecomer. This last, a patch-eyed fellow with a sailor's rolling gait, came hurrying along behind me.

The gatekeeper, as he barred the doors behind us, recited in a sort of doggerel the basic rules of the establishment. Between my own weariness and his thick country accent being unfamiliar to me, I failed to extract much of his meaning. This was no loss, for the laws were also posted beside an inner door, for the benefit of all guests who could read. Another small sign there announced the availability of tea and soup, in the canteen, for a charge of only a few pence; and I believe that if I had sworn myself penniless, nourishment and lodging would both have been provided gratis.

The man who ladled out the soup and poured the tea looked twice at me, and at my shilling thrice. But he took it and said nothing, and contrived to make my change, though no doubt he was seldom handed anything but coppers. I carried mug and bowl and spoon over to a heavy trestle table, dimly lighted but quite recently scrubbed clean. The one-eyed sailor perforce followed me, for all other furniture had been stacked or upended to make way for a recent mopping of the floor, which still shone damp.

The soup-man went away upon some chore, and we two were left alone in the large room. After tasting my soup, I passed it over to the sailor, in whose eyes I thought I could see the reflexive greed of those who live habitually near starvation. He was not reluctant to accept, and wolfed down the contents of my bowl even before beginning upon his own, perhaps in fear that I might change my mind.

It was natural enough, then, that we should begin to exchange a few words, and so my soup bought me a little information regarding the hostel to which I had been led by fate. I sat with my face mostly in the shadow of the distant lamp, pretending from time to time to sip a little tea. When we were finished in the canteen, we found ourselves assigned, as latecomers, not to the rows of ordinary cots which filled a long, dim dormitory room, but rather to an even older-looking chamber hard nearby. This room was smaller and even darker than the other, and in it the beds were not raised in the ordinary way. Rather they were thin pallets fixed right on the floor, and encased in bed-sized boxes, so that they looked like nothing so much as a row of coffins set out to accommodate the victims of some middle-sized disaster. The great majority of these beds were empty.

The disaster of which we were the victims was of

course the world—such was my dark thought as I looked upon the beds, and smelled the misery, and heard from the troubled sleepers in the next room almost continual groans, interspersed with strange prayers, oaths, and all the muttered illogic of bad dreams.

With my new companion I proceeded slowly along the row of bleak containers, of which we had our almost complete choice. The instinct that had drawn me to enter this place still held, and I still trusted in it, though as yet I could not see that it had helped me in the least. The sailor by now had begun to talk of the possibility of finding work along the docks, where no man was asked for his background or his papers. As I half-listened to him, my attention was captured by a curious fact: the odd receptacles before me were covered, one and all, with oilcloth, tightly sewn on. I squatted down beside one empty box to feel of the material, so very like that of my erstwhile prison rack.

The sailor had come to a stand beside the next coffin in the long row. Now he cackled, having put a perhaps natural misinterpretation upon my behavior. "Not quite yer silk or satin, is it, Matey?" He had promptly sized me up as one used to richer surroundings than these.

I stroked the fabric. "I was just wondering why they used this stuff?"

"Why?" He bent a little, to peer at me the better. "Why? 'Cause erlcloth won't offer a snug place t' no bugs. Wot did yer think?"

"In any case, I tolerate no such creatures about my person," I replied, absentmindedly fastidious. No doubt my voice contained more lordliness than appeared warranted by my situation.

"We-ell! I craves yer pardon most 'umbly, I'm sure,

Yer Grace. Or might it be Yer Worship, or jist wot?''
He felt strong, with my soup to fortify his belly.

But I was paying him very little attention. Holding in
one hand the thin blanket I had been issued upon leaving the canteen, I stepped into that strange bed as I
might have moved from a sinking ship into a lifeboat
that I did not expect would float. If I could not find here
the repose that I had so far been denied, I knew that I
must die with the first rays of dawn.

My neighbor meanwhile was stripping himself completely in preparation to retire. This seemed to be the
common practice here, judging by the clothes piled up
where other men were sleeping, doubtless on the old
theory that a bare skin is less attractive to vermin than
one snugly wrapped. I had limited my own undressing
to the removal of my cheap cloth cap; and now I noted
in passing that the long hair swinging before my eyes
had, since my heavy feeding, acquired a strong mixture
of youthful brown amid its gray.

There was no point in further hesitation, and quickly
I lay down, and quickly knew my doom. No sooner had
I willed to rest, than came again the quivering spasms
along the muscles of my arms, my back, my legs. To
turn in my bed, to stretch, to twist, to exert the full
power of my will, availed me nothing. I *could not* be
still. No matter what I did inside the oilcloth coffin, I
should never be allowed to rest.

Why, then, had my deepest instincts led me to this
strange bed? I sat upright and glared at it.

The sailor, now snugly blanket-wrapped in his own
box, appeared almost luxuriously comfortable. '' 'Is
Mightiness maybe finds the shape of 'is bed not to 'is
fancy? Har, har! Doss down in yer coffin like a brave
'un, Milord!''

I turned my gaze upon him, suddenly and with what

must have been an unexpected force, for he fell abruptly silent and shrank away, squinting narrowly at me with his one eye. Yet I was hardly aware of the fellow himself. It was the full unconscious meaning of his words that had struck me—aye, struck me!—with almost the impact of a second oaken cudgel, so that for several long seconds I could hardly move.

Lord . . . yes!

And coffin . . . yes!

But it was *my own coffin that I needed*, that I might find rest in my own homeland's holy soil!

With a single shock, the shards of my broken memory fell almost completely into place. I cast the poor thin blanket down and slowly stood erect, rising there amid the lost men, the gloom, the mumbled, hopeless prayers and curses, the fetor of illness and defeat.

Aye, "Your Grace" I once had been, indeed! And even higher honors than a dukedom had been mine. In my own land I had ruled as Prince, four hundred years and more before this fool who gibed at me was born!

The sailor crouched far down, then made as if to scramble from his box upon the side away from me. There must have been low growling in my throat, as I stepped from that false coffin. My long-nailed fingers must have worked, as if the man named Matthews and the still-nameless doctor were before me.

Where was my trunkful of good Transylvanian earth? It must long since have been unloaded from the ship, whose gangplank I had descended to the London dock . . . great heaven, how many unresting days ago? I had voyaged to England again, of course, because of . . .

"Mina!" I groaned aloud, casting the name of my beloved violently into that foul air. It was with relief sharp enough to be a shock that I realized in the next moment that my dear Mina must be quite safe, long miles away in Exeter. Her absence left me unencumbered for the war to come.

Oh, it was going to be a war, indeed! I knew not how many were against me, opponents clever, mysterious, and powerful. But the odds would not be all upon my enemies' side, although I fought alone. They were but breathing men, and I was vampire, immune to metal, knife or bullet; with the strength of twenty always in my sinews; capable during the hours of night of changing my form to that of an animal, or of a mist impalpable, and changing back again to man.

And no one in the world of 1897 had more experience of war than I—*Count Dracula.*

VI

As we rode from the docks back to our lodgings, Holmes maintained an irritable near-silence. Twice he began remarks upon extraneous subjects, but in each instance let his sentence die incomplete, and in such indifferent fashion that no reply seemed called for. This was so at variance with his customary manner of speech, and with his usual ability to divert his thoughts at will from professional matters, that it confirmed my impression of his having been profoundly disturbed by the riverfront murder.

"Holmes," I offered, with the idea of diverting him, "have you given any consideration to watching Her Majesty's Jubilee procession? There are people asking outrageous prices for the mere privilege of sitting an hour or two in a window of a room along the route. With half a dozen strangers as company, I suppose."

"Bah, I have no time," Holmes muttered. His tone was scarcely civil, and he continued to stare from the window of the cab as if hidden among the passers-by there were some arch-enemy who had just managed to escape him.

As we alighted from the cab in Baker Street, a ragged urchin darted toward Holmes from a nearby doorway, where he had evidently been in wait.

"Got yer message, sir," this small and rather unsavory person reported, giving his hatless forelock a touch that bore some resemblance to a military salute. "I been to the Northumberland, and neither the boots nor the maids remembers any particular gentleman wot would answer the description, sir."

"Well done, Murray." Holmes dropped coins into the grimy hand that shot out to accept them. "And what news of the dogs and rats?"

"Market in stray dogs is quite steady, sir. In rats—to tell the truth, I ain't been able to find out. None of me chums with connections along that line has been where I could discover 'em. I'll be going right off to 'ave another look."

Holmes dismissed the lad with a nod. When we had ascended to our rooms, I ventured to inquire whether the state of the market in dogs or rats might have any bearing upon any of his cases with which I was acquainted.

Stuffing his pipe with dark shag, Holmes only grunted in reply, and passed over to me without comment a visitor's card that had been left while we were out. The name it bore was that of Peter Moore, the American manufacturer of medical and scientific goods. The back bore a short written message:

Will call again in an hour or so. Am very anxious that everything possible be done to find John Scott.

After passing me the card, Holmes stood for a little while brooding out upon the warm spring afternoon beneath our window. Down in the street, children shouted in merriment over some game; a bird gave voice, and the sun shone warmly. The horror of the docks seemed to belong to another world, and shortly my friend managed to shake off the black mood that had threatened to engulf him, and turned to me with a small smile.

"My apologies, Watson. Your question is of course a fair one, and I only wish that I were certain of the answer. My thought is that the equipment belonging to Dr. John Scott can be of real use only to a medical experimenter. And, as we have seen, it is not logical that the items were stolen, with considerable risk, effort, and expense, in order to be sold. Then does it not follow that they were taken simply to be used?"

The murder had rather driven thoughts of Miss Sarah Tarlton's problem from my mind. "But by whom, Holmes? Surely none of the regular laboratories would stoop . . ."

"Of course they would not. But someone has. And if we can find out where these unknown experimenters are obtaining their subjects, we might be close to learning their identity and the nature of their work. So this morning I carried out a quick survey of all the legal, respectable suppliers of experimental animals in London, and convinced myself that none of them has lately enjoyed a marked increase in business.

"What, then, of the illegal or informal sources? To test them I dispatched young Murray, and several of his associates in this year's active corps of the Irregulars; with the results that have just given you cause to wonder."

Holmes knocked out his pipe into the fireplace, and reached for his violin. But before beginning to play, he faced me with a distant, abstracted look. "Has it occurred to you, Watson, that our two most recent cases have something in common?"

"The warehouse from which John Scott's things were removed is no great distance from the dock where the body of the unfortunate woman was found."

"True. But I had in mind a feature odder than mere geographical proximity."

"An involvement with out-of-the-ordinary medical materials."

Holmes nodded. "Precisely."

"Something of the sort did cross my mind," I admitted, then located a paper in my coat pocket, and brought it out. "Here is the copy you gave me of Peter Moore's inventory of the material taken from the warehouse. I have looked into it, and find no specific mention of any shirt like the one on the pier."

"Quite true." Gazing abstractedly past me, Holmes drew from his violin a thin, wild note. "But then Peter Moore did not have time to catalogue all the equipment before it was removed. Watson—"

"Yes?"

"Would a peculiar shirt of that type be likely to be of any use to a scientist studying plague?"

"In some cases, the victim may be driven to the maddest violence by delirium and excruciating pain."

"The human victim."

"Yes, of course."

Holmes put down his violin as abruptly as he had taken it up. "I find, Watson, that the time for concentrated mental effort has not yet arrived. Or perhaps I am simply not capable of it at the moment."

"My dear chap!"

"No, no, I am not ill. But this business of the killing

on the docks . . ." Once more Holmes let his words trail off.

"I can see it has affected you. Is it possible that you recognized the victim?"

"I did not."

"Do you think Lestrade will find the escaped madman he is looking for?"

"I trust he will." Never before had I heard such genuine fervor in Sherlock Holmes' voice when he was wishing his professional rivals success. "If he fails to do so . . . then I shall have to take a hand, in earnest. And I tell you, Watson, that I would rather not."

Holmes turned to face me directly as he spoke these last words, and in his speech and manner there was such an unusual depth of feeling that I stepped forward and laid a hand upon his arm. "I think it will be better, Holmes, for you to take a holiday. London in summer is not the most—"

"Bah!" He shook me off impatiently. "Do not talk to me now of holidays. Perhaps after this affair on the docks is settled." As if to himself he added: "Oh, but it is an offense to sanity."

"You mean the killer is insane? But that is surely not uncommon in a murderer."

"I do not mean the killer's motive; or not that alone." Holmes paused, looking at me as if with a kind of silent pleading.

At last I prompted: "I must say that the case of John Scott does not appear to me any plainer."

He smiled lightly. "Nor to me, as yet. But that is because that puzzle is incomplete. When I have more of the pieces in hand, I feel sure that they will fall together. But in the puzzle of the killing on the docks, I fear, Watson, that one of the pieces may be of the wrong shape. And what shall we make of that, hey?''

Holmes' manner was now grown positively feverish. Emotions I could not identify had him in their grip. ''And if the two cases should be connected, Watson, where does the connection stop? What if the whole world is destined to be the wrong shape, after all?''

I was now genuinely alarmed. ''Holmes, you must abandon this case at once. As your doctor, I insist that you must put it aside and rest.''

''No, Watson.'' What effort of will it may have cost him I shall never know, but in a few seconds my friend managed to appear fully in control of himself and as formidable as ever. ''With regard to other work, I shall take your advice. But it is absolutely impossible that I should abandon either of these two cases until they are solved, or until I am convinced at least that it is safe and proper for me to do so.''

As I stood in silence, not knowing what to think or do, Holmes, now looking perfectly normal, reached for his hat. ''I am going out,'' he said, ''to send a telegram or two to Plymouth, to try to learn if John Scott or his imitator has in fact taken ship from that port recently.'' He paused, looking at me with concern. ''All will be well, old fellow, I assure you.''

I shook my head. ''I wish I were as convinced of that as you seem to be at the moment.''

''Depend upon it.'' Holmes had never been more masterful.

I sighed. ''Then, if there is anything that I can do—''

''There on my desk, Watson, are the letters Scott sent to Miss Tarlton from Sumatra. I should be pleased to have your opinion of them. And there is one thing more.''

''You have but to name it.''

"I fear I stand in need of protection—no, not from my enemies this time, Watson, but from my friends—or, at any rate, my clients. In Miss Tarlton I sense the type, fortunately rare, who is only too anxious to assist the hired investigator; and Mr. Moore's note suggests that he shares this tendency. Such excessive zeal may be basically a result of American energy, but it is undoubtedly intensified by the fact that the young lady, at least, has no routine business to occupy her in London. So when they return here, separately or together, I ask you to consider them as your patients, suffering perhaps from anxiety, and to provide them with such attentions and reassurances as may keep them from taking any investigative action on their own, while I am at work upon the case."

"I see what you mean, Holmes, and of course I shall do the best I can. I wish I might hold out to them some hope."

"That John Scott still lives? It is a possibility, but I fear that in the end it will be no kindness to those who love him to present it to them as any more than that."

As soon as Holmes had gone, I picked up the small bundle of letters from his desk and settled myself in a chair with my back to the window. A few minutes spent pondering my friend's condition left me no wiser than before, and, after determining to keep a very close eye on him for further signs of trouble, I took up the top letter and began to read.

Skimming over those paragraphs which seemed irrelevant to the problem at hand—irrelevant except in that they demonstrated the existence of a stable, affectionate relationship between young Scott and Sarah Tarlton—I quickly located the few passages in the letters describing the scientist's pursuit of the animal that was supposed to spread the plague. There was no sensationalism in Scott's account; I thought that out of consideration for the girl's feelings he must have tried to minimize the dangers. Still his efforts at understatement could not conceal what a truly heroic achievement had been his, in the struggle through mountains, swamp, and jungle, all virtually unexplored, in the face of a thousand dangers and difficulties.

Success had at last crowned his efforts, and he had taken the animal he sought. I quote here a small portion of a letter written after he had first seen the creature, but before its capture:

> . . . the stories that reached me at home in which the beast was described as being a great ape, or ape-like, now seem certainly the result of some fabrication or misunderstanding, and I fear I have shipped a great deal of heavy equipment all the way to the South Seas for nothing, and have hired a dozen more porters than I would otherwise have needed. It has in fact the appearance and probably the habits of a giant rodent, larger perhaps than the tapir or the capybara.

This was certainly of interest, though as I read I could not see that it had any particular bearing upon Scott's subsequent disappearance. I worked my way doggedly through the pile of letters, looking especially for anything relating directly to the equipment taken from the warehouse. But of this I found scarcely another mention; an exception, in the last letter Miss Tarlton had received, was the following paragraph:

> . . . so there it was, safe in our nets at last, for all

its squealing and its snarls. Most of the men who had fled soon returned, and there was work for all hands. The first step of course was to take prophylactic measures against ourselves being infected with the plague, which we did with great thoroughness, as I had schooled the men. Now there is no need for you to be at all alarmed on my account, for the fine equipment that Pete and others have provided will let me bring the "critter" home quite safely for study and perhaps even for public exhibition later. I am sure it is of a species absolutely unknown to science until now. Thank God there cannot be many more like it upon the face of the earth; for if it were not under such good control as I will be able to establish, the animal would represent a terror and a potential weapon more fearful than the largest battleship.

Almost at the end of the same letter, I came across the passage to which Holmes had earlier referred:

. . . good news of another sort has come in via the native "grapevine." Another party of Americans or Europeans is said to be camped about ten miles away, on the banks of the Indragiri. I've sent an invitation for them to come for a visit, as I could use some company to share my triumph with.

I had just finished this last letter when a visitor was announced, who proved to be none other than Mr. Peter Moore. I had expected a man of middle age, but Mr. Moore was still on the youthful side of thirty-five. Well dressed in clothes of modern cut, dark-haired, and of a little more than middle height, he met me with a level though anxious gaze, and a fine manly handshake.

"Very pleased to meet you, Dr. Watson. Sarah tells me you seemed very sympathetic. But of course it's Mr. Holmes that I'm really anxious to talk to. To find out how I can best be of help. Is there any progress yet toward finding John?"

Despite the young man's open look and generally trustworthy appearance, and his evident anxiety, I felt it wisest in Holmes' absence not to discuss with anyone his thoughts on the matter. Therefore I countered Moore's question with one of my own. "How is Miss Tarlton? I see she has not come with you today."

"Sarah is . . . all right, I suppose." Moore gestured wearily. "As well as can be expected, given the burden that she bears. She's a very determined girl, and right now she's determined to control herself and simply wait, having finally put the case in Mr. Holmes' hands."

"I should say that her policy is a wise one."

"I'm sure it is. But I'm afraid I just don't have her patience. I had to let you gents know I'm ready and willing to do anything I can to help locate John."

"Is this your first visit to London, Mr. Moore?"

"Oh, no. My mother's family is English, or was."

We had arrived at what might have become something of an awkward pause, when to my relief a distraction arrived in the form of Mrs. Hudson, who announced a second visitor. "It's Inspector Lestrade, sir."

"By all means show him in."

The Inspector's face was rather more animated, and less strained, than it had been when Holmes and I left him standing on the pier a few hours earlier. He entered carrying in his hand a large canvas bag, of a kind I had previously seen used to hold evidence. There was something hard and solid inside, for the bag made a substantial sound when Lestrade set it down. I assured him that Holmes would very likely be back in a matter of minutes, and that it was quite all right for him to wait. I introduced Mr. Peter Moore as a friend of another client, dropping by to volunteer his services.

"Oh, ah!" said Lestrade. "Please to meet you, sir. You've nothing to do, then, with the business on the docks—so I can speak freely. I don't mind telling you both, gentlemen, that I don't know how Mr. Holmes does it—but he does. Mr. Moore, if your friend requires a miracle, I'd say he or she has come to the right shop."

"What is it, Lestrade?" I asked.

"Why, the oddity, just as Mr. Holmes predicted. I was lucky enough to be able to get divers on the job within a matter of minutes after you'd left. And on the bottom of the Thames they found this bag." Stooping to open the canvas container, Lestrade brought out of it another bag, which if unfolded would have been even larger than the first. "And containing these."

As he spoke, Lestrade undid the fastenings of the inner bag. Metal clashed as he let its contents slide out upon the carpet. There lay before us two pairs of heavy manacles, circles of steel connected by short, strong chains. "Darbies and leg-irons, I make them out to be, though they're a good deal different from the style we use at the Yard. I've got people at work already trying to trace 'em. Especially made, I'd say, and extra strong. As you see, both pair are locked. The keys are missing."

Peter Moore came near to shouldering me aside when Lestrade displayed his find. I looked at the young American in surprise, but quickly forgot my ruffled feelings when I beheld the strange expression of excitement on his face.

For a few moments Moore seemed unable to find words or even gestures to express his thoughts. Then he seized one set of the manacles and held them up. There were only a few spots and traces of rust on the bright steel, which could not have been long in the river.

"These were made by my company in New York," Peter Moore burst out. "And they were with John in the South Seas."

VII

Stepping on shaky legs from that droll imitation of a coffin, I knew that I had recovered my identity not an hour too soon to save my life.

Nowhere but in the hallowed soil of my homeland would I, vampire, be able to find rest. Turning impulsively to the cowed sailor, I barked out: "Tell me! Where shall the unclaimed baggage be taken, from a ship unloading at the East India docks?" Of course I had in mind the great leather trunk that had accompanied me to England; besides containing large sums of money, my own clothing, and papers of identification under several names, it was half full of that sweet stuff I needed more than air.

Huddling in mute fright, the man could only shake his head. Of course there was no reason why he should have known anything about baggage-handling procedures, or what had happened to my trunk. Nor had I myself the least idea of where to begin a search; so it was indeed fortunate for my hopes of survival that during my London visit six years earlier I had taken certain measures with the idea of establishing a permanent residency.

Never mind how foolish those ambitions of mine were proven when the pack of vampire-hunters fastened on my trail; I have told that story elsewhere. The point was that some at least of those scattered, secret nests I had then built for myself, and lined with imported earth, must be still intact after no more than six years—or so I devoutly hoped, as I stalked out of that noisome dormitory toward the main doors of the hostel.

As I drew near those doors my purpose of departure must have been obvious, for the gatekeeper at once emerged from some cubbyhole nearby. He was a large man, garbed now in a blanket that he had draped about him like a toga, and evidently accustomed to peculiar midnight fits among his clientele. In a voice heavy with authority he warned me that the doors were going to stay locked and barred until daylight.

"Just toddle back t' bed now, like a good chap. Wot business you 'as out there will keep till—whoa!"

Quite gently I set him out of my path, for they were good Christian folk who operated the shelter, and they had served me well—aye, better than they knew. I threw the bar aside, and bent my waning strength, one hand to push and one to pull, upon the lock. It was strong, but not to be classed with those gorilla-manacles. Presently I heard the splintering of old wood, and could feel metal bend beneath my fingers. To pay for the damage I tossed a gold sovereign behind me as I left, and I silently vowed a future donation upon a grander scale.

The greasy fog had grown even thicker. A few paces along the street, away from the flaring gaslight, and I was out of human ken. A silent pause of a few moments was required, in which to reorganize my restored powers; then in the form of bat I let the pavement drop away beneath my feet, and sought the free winds of the higher air.

Once risen past the heaviest of the mist, I took my bearings from the stars, and set a course to the south-west. In my estimation the best hidden of my caches deposited in 1891 lay beneath the floor of a disused stable, behind a house in Bermondsey.

Even in bat-form, I could still feel the back of my head throbbing from that accursed bludgeon-blow. Whose arm had held the wood that struck it? Whilst flying over the river I could not help but look for one particular large rowboat among the myriad craft that lined the wharves; but of course any such search would have been hopeless, even without the heavy, swirling London fog which grew but deeper and chiller as the night wore on.

Nor could I guess which of the shrouded buildings was the one in which I had been held a prisoner—I only knew it must be somewhere near the water. Nor had I any idea where to begin a search for the blond, arrogant young doctor, whose nameless face burned in my memory. Nor for Matthews, nor for the "other lads" who served the same infamous cause, whatever it might be. Perhaps, I mused, I would have to begin by tracking down the shadowy Barley, who " 'ad 'opes" of being able to furnish the evildoers with something that they needed—before June 22, which date meant nothing to me.

There was of course another associate of the plotters whose name and face had been left in my possession. Sally, though a dweller in the abyss of poverty and crime, had suffered torture and risked death in trying to set me free, and thereby had established a claim upon my honor as great as any the greatest and most lovely queen on earth could ever have created. Now I should never be able to go peaceably about my own affairs

until I had avenged Sal's injuries as well as my own,
and had done all I could to see her through the whole
affair in safety. The recent incident on the pier had gone
some way toward accomplishing these goals; it had
been, however, no more than a good beginning. But
before planning the satisfaction of honor, I must first
make sure of my own survival.

Whilst crossing the river I remarked to myself upon
the changes that had in six short years so altered London's face. There was of course the continuing prolif-
eration of electric lights. And there were the two newly
complete bridges, Lambeth and Tower. Stretched
across one of these was a vast banner:

VR 1837   1897 VR
    The love of all thy sons encompass thee
    The love of all thy daughters cherish thee
    The love of all thy people comfort thee

Of course, VR, Victoria Regina, '37 to '97—the
grand old queen had reigned for sixty years, and her
people who had grown to love her held Jubilee again as
in '87 . . . I remembered reading about that, in preparation for my first visit.

London's vast murmuring voice, now muted by the
lateness of the hour and by the fog, but never really
stilled by day or night, rose to greet me as I descended
to the south bank. The roof-slates of Bermondsey were
soon beneath my leathery wings, and I had no difficulty
in finding Leathermarket Street.

To my consternation it was soon apparent that
change had struck closer to home, for me, than Tower
Bridge. The house and grounds which had so admirably
suited me in 1891 had obviously passed since then to

different ownership. The occupants I recalled were an elderly, moribund couple, unshakably settled into routine, and far too dim of sense to pay the least attention to my comings and goings by day or night. But the place was now inhabited—I should perhaps say garrisoned—by a vast and evidently insomniac family, who had a snoring reserve quartered in every upstairs bedroom, whilst even now, long past midnight, their main body held noisy carousal on the main floor.

In the face of this bedlam I did not even land, but flew away again without bothering to try the stable, from whence sounded not only the snorts of restive horses, but the half-smothered laughter of some lickerish kitchen wench. I considered that I still had strength enough to fly on to my next cache, in Mile End, and, if conditions there should somehow prove even more inhospitable, fly back again. Or I might try Carfax, the estate I had so briefly occupied in 1891, whose large, wild grounds I thought must still hold hospitable soil. That was in Purfleet, a suburb to the north . . . .

The tide was turning now, making my passage over running water smooth and easy. North of the river again, I found to my relief that in a poorer neighborhood change had been less. The tiny Mile End churchyard that I sought was to all appearances unaltered. Six years previous, by what stratagems and strivings I need not relate here, I had interred in this place a coffin-sized box half-filled with my own rich imported graveyard earth; I had trusted that here it would remain hidden, one alien leaf in the midst of an English forest.

My trust was justified. Wraith-like I now melted into the ground, found the box just where I had buried it,

and inside it resumed man-shape. My body rested—
rested, ah!—upon the soft soil of my homeland. A
blessed peace bathed my tormented limbs, and awareness faded utterly from my exhausted brain.

VIII

Lestrade, Peter Moore, and I were still standing around the oilcloth bag, and the surprise with which we gazed at its contents and at each other was still fresh, when a ring at the bell was followed by the delivery of a telegram. The message was from Holmes himself, addressed to me:

AM ON A FRESH TRAIL. WILL TRY TO RETURN TONIGHT, BUT NO CAUSE FOR CONCERN IF I DO NOT. S.H.

Even as I finished reading this aloud, the inspector voiced his suddenly developed suspicions regarding Peter Moore: "If you're asking me to believe, Dr. Watson, that this gentleman is just visiting here upon some other business entirely, when I just happen to bring in these darbies, and he just happens to be the man who made 'em—well, no policeman worth his badge is going to accept that sort of thing as a coincidence."

"Accept it or not, as you choose," Moore answered, with some irritation. "I tell you, my firm built these restraints, and I saw them packed off with John Scott to Sumatra. And I saw them again—either these very items, or others from the same lot—less than a month ago, in a warehouse here in London."

Lestrade's gaze, fixed on the young American, grew

sharper than ever. "I should like to know, sir, just what connection your business with Mr. Holmes has with a certain murder that I have under investigation."

Moore returned Lestrade's gaze stonily. "A murder? As far as I know, there is no connection at all."

"Then you would have no objection to discussing with the police the business that has brought you to Mr. Holmes?"

"As a matter of fact, I have already tried to do so." Moore's irritation had grown to anger. "Yesterday morning Miss Sarah Tarlton and I were at Scotland Yard, doing our best to impress the men there with the importance of the matter. It is not our fault that we were put off."

Lestrade was silenced for the moment. I took the opportunity to outline for him the problem of the missing American physician and his equipment. The inspector listened intently, and I judged that again a new evaluation of the case—of both cases, which now seemed more than ever to be connected—was developing in his mind.

When I was done, Peter Moore inquired: "See here, I now seem to be the only one present who knows only half the story. What is this murder you keep speaking of? Who was killed, and by whom? Is there any evidence that John Scott might have been in any way involved?"

"I don't see him as the killer at all, sir," Lestrade answered. "The man who took the things from the warehouse was a cool customer, if nothing else, while our killer's an absolute maniac if there ever was one. But *some* connection there must be. . . . Mr. Moore, I apologize in the name of Scotland Yard, for not giving your problem the attention it undoubtedly deserves. Now if you and this young lady, Miss . . ."

"Sarah Tarlton. She and John were engaged to be married."

"Ah, yes. Now if you and I were to go and call at Miss Tarlton's hotel, do you suppose that she would be willing to come along to the Yard with us and tell her story again? I'll give my solemn word that this time she'll be listened to."

"I'm sure Sarah will agree, if it will help to find him."

Carrying off his oilcloth bag of evidence in one hand, while the other rested in most friendly fashion on the arm of Peter Moore, Lestrade very soon bade me good-bye. I stood for a moment at the window, and watched the two men get into a four-wheeler.

It was to be a busy evening at Baker Street. Scarcely had I finished my solitary dinner, when two visitors were announced. Once again Sarah Tarlton and Peter Moore entered our sitting room, this time together. Both were badly upset, and Miss Tarlton in particular was almost speechless with indignant rage. It did not take me long to learn the cause.

"Oh, Dr. Watson, that dreadful little man! We had been talking to him in his office for five minutes before I got the drift of his questions . . . oh, it makes my blood boil to think of it! He suspects John of . . . oh, I can't talk about it!"

Moore, himself pale but much less distraught than the young lady, alternately held her hand and patted her arm, with a concern perhaps something more than merely friendly. "It was just as Sarah says, Dr. Watson. The inspector wouldn't come right out and say so, but I'm sure this sudden interest of the police in finding John is only because they suspect him of being—involved—in this horrible murder. As I understand it, they think some violent patient of his must have escaped . . . it's really completely stupid. Where's Mr. Holmes? Is he ever coming back?"

Suddenly Miss Tarlton's anger was temporarily exhausted, and she trembled on the verge of tears. "If only they would simply *look* for John—I keep picturing them shooting him down like a dog, on sight. . . ."

Glad to be able at last to say something genuinely helpful, I hastened to reassure her that the Metropolitan Police were not generally in the habit of carrying firearms (though I knew that Lestrade for one was seldom without his pocket pistol), let alone discharging them promiscuously at suspects. When I had repeated my assurances several times Miss Tarlton seemed at last willing to believe them, but her general anxiety for her fiance was scarcely abated.

She dabbed at her eyes. "Dr. Watson, we are abusing your kindness, taking up your time. . . ."

"Not at all. Not a bit."

"Did Mr. Holmes seem *hopeful* when he went out? Have you *no* idea at all when he'll be back?"

"Hopeful? That would be difficult to say," I replied. "I do not even know whether the fresh trail he mentions in his telegram is connected with Dr. Scott's case or some other. As to when he will return, I speak from long experience when I say it may not be till morning, or even later."

Peter Moore pressed the girl's hand again. "Come along now, Sarah. I'll see you back to the hotel."

"I will not be soothed and quieted!" she burst out.

"Not while they are hunting John, who may be out there somewhere, needing me! He could be ill or dying—God, how can I simply rest?"

"Sarah, you must save your strength. If later—"

"Never mind later, they are hunting him now. Peter, I am going to go back to Scotland Yard and wait. If John is brought in I'll be there. After coming all the way across the Atlantic, I am not going to be sent off like a child to bed. You may go to your hotel and rest if you are tired."

There followed some five minutes' dispute between the two, which I found rather embarrassing. Moore's angry pleas and arguments had no more effect upon the lady's determination than did the milder protests which I, at intervals, dared to interject. At last I judged it would be wiser to comply with her ideas as far as I reasonably could, and shortly all three of us were in a cab and headed for Scotland Yard. It seemed to me that her return visit there would be less difficult for all concerned if I were present to act as intermediary; I was well known in those precincts after so many years as Holmes' associate. His parting instructions were, of course, also fresh in my mind.

Our old acquaintance Tobias Gregson was, as I soon found out, the detective in charge of tracing all connections between the Scott case and the Grafenstein killing, while his old rival Lestrade continued to direct the overall search for the murderer.

Gregson, tall, stooped, and fair, quite courteously led the two young Americans to a comfortably furnished anteroom where, as he said, they were welcome to wait, and where any fresh news of John Scott would be brought to them at once. Then the detective beckoned me away, asking for a word in private. As soon as we were alone, I detected something like triumph in his pale face.

"Well, Dr. Watson, I suppose Mr. Holmes is close on the heels of some suspect in the killing?"

"I am sure he is very busy."

"But not on the brink of a solution?"

"Not to my knowledge."

"Then, Doctor, I'd just like you to hear this."

So saying, Gregson led me along a narrow corridor. Stopping before a plain door, my guide motioned me to silence, and then opened a small spyhole in the door, indicating with a gesture that I should look in. The room revealed was large enough to hold on one of its walls a vast map of London, and a couple of policemen seated with their backs toward me. In another chair, facing the spyhole, sat an emaciated old man, wrapped from his shoulders down in a prison blanket which he kept clutched about him.

"And is that your mad killer, Gregson?" I asked, closing the judas window and turning away.

"Him?" The detective laughed softly. "Not by a long way. No, he's charged only with stealing a blanket—not the one he has wrapped about him now, but one he pinched through an open window in Whitechapel. Nor has he the least idea that a murder's under investigation. But I think you and Mr. Holmes are both going to be mighty interested in what he has to say."

Gregson opened the door and we both went in. The old man, who by his speech and manners gave the impression of belonging to the lower classes, looked up briefly startled, and then went on with what he had been saying:

"I tells you gentlemen, I took that bit o' cloth only in

the name o' common decency, and meanin' to bring it back in the morning when the shops and stalls opened, and I could buy some proper clothes.''

Bit by bit, under the prodding questions of the policemen, the man's story came out, interspersed with his objections at being made to repeat it to them once again. The essence of his account was that he had reached into someone's window for the blanket only because he had been compelled, during the night, to sell almost all the clothing he had been wearing to a stranger. The mysterious man who had forced him into the transaction under threat of bodily harm had then paid him for his rags with gold.

''Oh, come off it, now!'' Gregson's voice was suddenly thick with convincing doubt. He picked up an envelope from a desk in the center of the room, and slid a gold coin out of it into his hand. ''You stole this sovereign just as you stole the blanket. Now didn't you?''

''I never! Nossir! Beggin' yer pardon, sir, but I sold my clothes for that. Sold 'em fair, I did, and I was just a-borryin' the blanket to see me over until—''

''Yes, yes. Let's hear just once again *how* you came to sell your clothes. Who bought 'em?''

The man unburdened himself of a hopelessly weary sigh. ''You've 'eard all that.''

''The good doctor here hasn't,'' Gregson prodded, meanwhile casting a faintly triumphant glance in my direction. ''Now, once more, if you please.''

''Well, sir.'' The old man sighed again, this time resignedly. ''It were this 'ere madman, like.''

''Who?''

''Lor' bless you, sir, I didn't know 'im. And I wish I may never see the like of 'im again. Stark nekkid 'e was—talk of decency! Grip like a vise 'e 'ad, I swear.

106

And 'is eyes—I don't like t' think on 'em, and that's a fact.''

The old man was now warming somewhat to the repetition of the tale, which after all earned him the respectful attention from an assemblage of persons who may perhaps have seemed to him important. ''The madman? I'll tell you. Myke a noise, says 'e, and the next noise 'eard in this 'ere street'll be the crunch o' yer bones a-breakin'. 'Ere, tyke this coin, 'e says, a-'oldin' up that wery sovereign, an' toss me over yer rags. An' I tossed 'em over, sir—you would, too, an' that's the Lord's truth. An' bless me if 'e didn't pay me, just as 'e said 'e would.''*

---

*I said in an earlier chapter that I would return to this point later, and now seems as good a time as any.

Those who think me unlikely to pay fairly, even generously, for goods got from the innocent do not know me. They know only the stories told by my enemies and their dupes, from my breathing days in the 15th century, through the 19th when Van Helsing concocted his lurid lies, down to the present. As if by some law of social entropy, when one's reputation changes, the change is almost always for the worse; and five centuries of life give time for a great deal of change.

That my name is ever going to improve again must be considered problematical at best, but at least its past deterioration can be charted. Let the serious students of 15th century affairs assure more casual readers that in my breathing days, as Prince of Wallachia, I was accused by some of being *too scrupulously honest.* Certain troublemakers, dissidents in my realm, groaned that I expected *too much* in the way of trustworthiness from my subjects!

Of course it was not the merchants who so charged me; *they* did not find the stench of robbers' bodies, staked up beside my roads as admonition, too much for their nostrils. Nor was it my country's peasants, or any of its honest poor, who launched the legend of my unexampled deviltry. When I ruled, their doors could stay unbarred by night, whilst their wives and daughters walked abroad in peace and safety. I am, and was, a strong-willed man; else were I dead, five hundred years ago, from sword-wounds at the hands of my less loyal subjects. The troublemakers claimed to find unbearable the mere rumors that issued from the dungeons underneath my castles, where I had those who preyed upon the innocent conveyed as speedily as possible; nor did nobility of blood preserve them from my justice. But all this is as a story that is told. —Dracula.

A door opened behind me, and Lestrade came quietly into the room, a gleam of suppressed excitement in his eye. He exchange a cryptic glance with Gregson, who quietly went out. After a nod to me, Lestrade, who had evidently heard the old man's story at least once before, took over the questioning.

"Now, dad, just where did this strange encounter of yours with the naked man take place?"

" 'Twas in Upper Swandam Lane, yer honor."

"And when?"

"Long 'bout the middle o' last night."

Lestrade placed two fingers, close together, upon the huge map of London that occupied one wall. "Upper Swandam Lane, Doctor, and right here's the pier where the, er, evidence was found." To the witness: "What did this strange man look like, apart from not being dressed?"

The fellow in the chair looked from one of us to the other. "Well, he were a sight taller than either of you gentlemen. Lean enough so that 'is ribs stuck out. But not wasted nor feeble; strong as an ox, 'e was."

"Dark or fair? Young or old?"

"Well, 'e was gray, or partly so."

All this description, I noted to myself, tallied well with Holmes' account of the man who had worn the shirt.

Lestrade pressed on. "Any sign that this chap had been shot? Wounded?"

"Huh! Not 'im!"

After another question or two, Lestrade beckoned me to follow him out into the corridor. Gregson was there, and with him a one-eyed, rascally-looking fellow, accoutered in some of the garments of a sailor. This man the detectives introduced to me as "Jones," one of the most valuable informers in the pay of the

CID. I remember thinking that the pay of an informer must be modest indeed, for this man appeared not much this side of starvation.

Jones' story, which he repeated in a rough and hurried whisper at the request of the detectives, was that he had been last night at the Salvation Army shelter on Sidney Street, where he had witnessed an incident so incredible that he had decided it must be brought directly to Lestrade's attention; though not until this evening, I gathered, had the inspector been receptive to his story.

The informer was carrying with him a ragged, dirty cloth cap, which he said had been left behind at the shelter by an incredibly strong man. This individual had spoken to Jones there, had shared his soup and tea, and then had suddenly jumped up out of his bed and departed. At midnight the doors were kept locked, but the man had forced them open barehanded. This was such a display of strength that, as Jones put it, he would hesitate to describe it to us, were it not that the shattered wood and metal must be still available as evidence. The patrolman on the beat had been summoned to the shelter, and his report would doubtless be coming through channels.

Lestrade nodded. "Yes, you did well to tell us. Let me see the cap."

With it in hand, Lestrade went into a small, dusty storeroom, from which he emerged a few minutes later with two more, almost as old and worn, but each of a different cut and color. Taking all three together in his hand, he led us back to the door of the room in which the elderly witness was being questioned.

Opening the spy-hole, Lestrade gestured for the informer to look through. "Was it him?"

"No sir, not much likeness at all," came the quick

answer. "Same general build, is all. This one looks quite feeble. The other—very weak he was, I *don't* think! If you doubts my word on that, sir, you'd better go along and look at those hostel doors."

"I suppose I had. But there's just a bit more to do here, first." Bringing me with him—Jones stayed in the outer darkness of the corridor—Lestrade re-entered the interrogation room.

The witness was now somewhat more at ease; an older constable, with hair as gray as his own, had come in to talk and joke with him. Lestrade in turn now jollied him along a bit, and, when he had put his man as much at ease as possible, presented him with the three caps, asking him to choose which was the one he had sold to the naked stranger.

After only the smallest hesitation, the old man selected the cap that the informer had brought with him.

When Lestrade and I were out in the hall again, he turned in my direction, looking positively gleeful. "And now I had really better visit the hostel, where the trail is going to be hottest. Dr. Watson, I think you can tell Mr. Sherlock Holmes that this is one case in which his theories are not going to be needed, and the plain evidence in the hands of the police is quite sufficient."

I murmured some reply, that was perhaps no more courteous than it had to be. A minute later I had re-joined my two companions, and shortly after that the three of us were on our way back to Baker Street, Miss Tarlton having at last been persuaded that the search for John Scott was giving no sign as yet of bearing fruit.

She stubbornly insisted, however, on coming on to Baker Street to see if Sherlock Holmes were yet at home. "Then I promise, Dr. Watson, that we will cease to bother you—oh, but you have been a great help and comfort to me tonight.''

I found my annoyance melting.

As the cab drew up before our rooms, I could see that they were dark. Miss Tarlton had just admitted, with some reluctance, that it was time to call an end to the day's adventures, and I had just got down from the cab and turned to bid the two young people goodnight, when from behind me sounded a soft shuffling of naked feet upon the pavement. I turned to confront the shabby figure of young Murray.

The boy's eyes were excitedly alight. "Dr. Watson, sir? Will Mr. Holmes be back soon?''

"I cannot say.''

"Well, sir, when 'imself is not available, I'm to give to you, privately, any important news I should discover.''

Murray's dancing eyes made it superfluous to ask whether he had at present any news he considered of importance. After a moment's thought I signed to the people in the cab to wait, and drew the lad aside. As soon as I had heard his information, I led him back to where the others waited. "Tell these people,'' I ordered, ''what you have just told me.''

"Well sir—ma'm—two hours ago I was at Barley's—that's in Soho, a public house, and famous for their sporting entertainments. It seemed to me a likely place to find out who's been buyin' rats, for they has thousands in their show—and there was a man there just answered the description of this Dr. Scott that Mr. Holmes is lookin' for. And I heard Barley 'imself say to this man, 'Doctor.' ''

Miss Tarlton emitted a little gasp, compounded of equal parts of fear and joy. I wished with all my heart that Holmes were present, but he was not. Peter Moore and I looked at each other, in prompt and silent agreement that we had better go at once to Barley's. And I suppose we both knew from the beginning that there would be no hope of persuading Miss Tarlton to stay away.

IX

When I sank gratefully into slumber in my snug earthen den, it was with the expectation of sleeping the earth's rotation fully around. In this estimate I was not far wrong; nothing short of an attempt to stake me through the torso could have roused me much sooner. When the first crack of consciousness broke into my dreamless oblivion, I could feel that the bulk of the planet had turned between me and the sun, and a clock somewhere nearby was striking ten. I awoke hungry, but otherwise greatly refreshed in mind and body. Even the pain in the back of my head had dwindled to the point of being scarcely noticeable.

Some six feet underground lay my comparatively new box. It was half-filled, of course, with hospitable homeland soil, and wedged between the remnants of two old wooden coffins, whose peaceful tenants were far past objecting to their restless new neighbor, although his installation had nudged them into postures far from dignified. Not that my clandestine digging had wrought havoc any worse than that of the breathing gravediggers in their sunlit routine. Fortune for once had smiled on me indeed, in that my den lay undisturbed. Below my six-years-planted box, round it on every side, and now above it too, the soil was thick with jumbled old bones, churned up by the sextons in their ceaseless search for space in which to plant the recent dead. In a long rush hour that goes on and on, the London cemeteries were—for all I know still are—more crowded than the streets above, a circumstance that the silent majority of the population are in no condition to protest.

Like smoke I rose to the dank air from my small borrowed plot. In the shadow of a half-fallen shed nearby, a brace of large rats tarried unwisely to observe my assumption, above ground, of the form of man. When I had called them to me, they provided all the material nourishment* I really needed at the moment. Yet I found I had the appetite for more; and with this goal in mind, I began to walk from the churchyard, down one of the darker byways of Mile End.

My normal hunting methods bear little resemblance to those of breathing men; the great control I am able to exercise over the lower orders of life obviates the need to stalk, or to kill from a distance. On this occasion I had not gone far before there harkened to my silent siren song a single large black rat, of glossy coat and graceful form. The race of *Rattus rattus* had even at that time been much diminished in most European cities, more by the effective warfare of his larger brown cousin the Norway rat *(Rattus Norvegicus)* than by the immemorial efforts of men, dogs, and cats.

---

*I had better pause here to make it clear to modern readers misled by the wild tales of my enemies, that human gore is *not* my customary food. The delight that I seek from women's veins is frankly sexual. But for sustenance, the blood of any mammalian species will serve my modest needs; it is my belief that most of any vampire's really essential nourishment comes from some mysteriously penetrating emanation of the Sun. Full sunlight is too much for us, of course, as breathing men will drown in a short time in a surplus of the same water that they must have to drink.

As bold as a bandit, though he could no more overcome my mental grip than he could have fought free of my hands, black *rattus* looked me in the eye and bared an ivory tooth, and I had not the heart to take his blood for a mere whim of appetite. So I stood there in the dark, holding and stroking him like a pet, and meanwhile let my thoughts begin to turn on deeper subjects.

Of course my waylaying at dockside had not been the work of anyone who knew my true identity. The ways in which they had tried to murder me—their carelessness in letting me get free after such efforts—their puzzlement at my vampirish blood—all these were proof enough of that. No, only the bitch-goddess Fortune had picked me as their victim, to serve their evil experiments, experiments that I still did not understand. . . . Well, when I had found the villains out, they would live just long enough to rue their choice of prey.

As I stood there petting my black rat, and nursing blacker thoughts, I became aware of some folk approaching along an alley. Three pairs of feet were coming, those of young men or boys nearly grown. One of them was carrying—something—that both squirmed and squealed, in half a dozen subhuman voices. Presently the walkers rounded a corner and came into my sight—though I was still not in theirs—and I perceived that the squeals emanated from a canvas bag alive with captured rodents.

My curiosity aroused, I remained standing where I was whilst they drew closer. Surely, I thought, they are not taking rats for food? Poverty was all about me in this part of London, but I had not seen starvation of the sort that comes with an extended siege, and argues breathing folk into trying the taste of rats.

The three youths were almost near enough to bump me, before one of them spied or heard something, and quickly flicked open the shade of a tin lantern. After their first startlement at seeing me in its uncertain beams, my wretched clothing acted in my favor, reassuring my discoverers that I was lower, if anything, in the social scale than they.

" 'Ere, mate!" one cried out. "Fair give me a turn, you did, standin' there in the dark like that. Wotcher got—well, pickle me if it ain't a pet."

"Just lookit 'im," another chimed in, "a-strokin' of it like a bloody kitten!"

I held out the quiet rat toward them in one hand. "It is yours, if you like, to go with those you have already."

As I might have expected, my accent, upperclass and foreign-flavored, undid some of the reassurance of my clothes. The one who held the lantern asked me: "Not sick, is it?"

"My pet here? Not a bit." In the same moment I shifted the grip of my fingers, and released that of my mind. In my hand the little beast became a blur of motion, ready to bite the flesh that its jaws could no longer reach, now that I held it by the neck. After a moment, another youth unslung his sack and held it out, and in the black one went.

"Tell me," I asked, "what will you do with them?"

They glanced at one another. "Look 'ere—you ain't in the business?"

"I am not, but I might be. Oh, I would prefer to be not your competitor, my friends, but your associate." The smell of rats burned in the air, and forced my thoughts back to that grotesque, improbable laboratory. Ah, to be free of honor's claims! Could such a wish be honorably made, I would have prayed it then. In Exeter, Mina was waiting, who for six years had been more dear to me than life itself, and whom I had not seen in almost all that time. Yet honor held me in London, to fight a war. "I can catch rats, as you have seen. Where are they needed?"

They at first were loath to tell me where their market was. So from the holes and crevices I coaxed out a dozen more rats, some black, some brown, which performance filled their bag to squirming tautness with very little effort on their part. Then soon I learned the young men had more bags, and cages, aboard a cart nearby and waiting to be filled. No more rats appeared, however, until I had been made full partner in the enterprise.

"Thruppence a head we're gettin', mate, and it's share and share alike when we divvy up."

"Those terms seem fair. And we are selling the rats to—?"

They looked at one another, shrugged. One spoke: "No more than one steady market, these days, chum. It's Barley's."

X

During our drive to Soho, some firm words from both Peter Moore and myself succeeded in persuading Sarah Tarlton that when we reached Barley's she must remain in the cab while we two men went inside. The appearance of a young woman of her class in such a place at such a time must cause the kind of sensation which, if we were to have any opportunity of surprising our quarry, it was essential to avoid. Then too, by remaining outside and on watch, she would be able to observe all who left the place or entered.

"If I see John," she announced, "I am going straight to him, no matter what."

"Of course." Peter Moore was looking at her earnestly, and again holding her hand. "But you had better be sure. If it is instead a man who only looks like John, then leave him to Dr. Watson and me."

"I'll be sure, Peter. Have no doubts about that." Her gaze, feverish with anxiety, was already busy darting this way and that among the passersby. "Oh, if only we can find him before those policemen do!"

At my orders the cabman stopped across the street from Barley's, where I directed him to wait. Murray jumped down nimbly from the seat beside the driver, to lead the way; and Moore and I followed, joining the intermittent stream of men now entering the public house. Before leaving Baker Street I had gone up to my room, and now I could feel inside my coat the reassuring bulge of my old service revolver.

The ground-floor parlor, which we entered first, was a large room filled with the fumes of drink and tobacco, where a wide-shouldered, hearty, mustached man of middle age presided behind the bar. This individual obviously had many friends among the patrons, and after a few moments spent listening to the exchange of rough, good-humored talk, I understood that this was Barley himself. His friends, and indeed the crowd in general, were an inclusive mixture of all the classes of the metropolis. A few were well-dressed, and undoubtedly gentlemen, while others were the basest ruffians. Of the female sex only a very small number were present, and these exclusively of the lowest class. I noticed particularly one girl who would have been pretty, even striking, had not one side of her face been almost covered by a great, disfiguring strawberry birthmark. This girl was subject to rude treatment as she endeavored to push her way through the crush, as if in search of someone; and I was well satisfied that we had persuaded Sarah Tarlton to remain outside.

Moore and I ordered drinks, and in general tried to give the impression of a pair of sportsmen out for a night's amusement. Meanwhile we of course were keeping both eyes open for the man we had come to find. I was distracted almost at once, however, by a chance encounter with an old acquaintance.

"Why, it *is* John Watson. Shouldn't have thought it likely to meet you in a place like this."

I turned to behold a dark-haired, handsome man, but little changed, save for the addition of a pair of spectacles, in the three or four years since I had seen him last. "Why, Jack Seward! Nor I you, if it comes to that." Eight or nine years younger than I, Seward had first entered the circle of my acquaintances some fifteen years earlier, when he was a dresser in the surgery at Bart's. I was aware that in the last seven or eight years he had risen rapidly, and when last I met him he had become a specialist in mental illness and was in charge of an asylum at Purfleet.

Seward explained that he had come to Barley's chiefly at the request of a friend of his; this was a tall and rather taciturn gentleman at his side, whom he called Arthur and then introduced to us as Lord Godalming. His Lordship had with him a brace of terriers, one of which he held and petted like a child. These he had brought along, as he put it, to see how they might do; other blood sports were out of season and angling had not yet begun.

"And are you still in charge at the asylum?" I inquired, making conversation, while simultaneously managing—as I prided myself—to keep nearly the whole room under observation.

"Oh, yes—damned drafty old place—more room than we need for the patients, but that's as well at present." Seward removed his spectacles and squinted rather nearsightedly around the room. "Have some guests in from Exeter, to see the Jubilee."

There was some question, it seemed, of the dogs being weighed in and examined in advance of their call to enter the pit for combat, and Lord Godalming and Dr. Seward soon bade us a temporary farewell and took the small, nervous animals upstairs, a development I rather welcomed as giving me a freer hand for business.

The chief decorations of Barley's parlor were glass cases, each containing one or more stuffed dogs. Every preserved animal was labeled with its name, and the dated record of some no doubt remarkable number of rats it had killed in the pit within a specified interval of time. I noticed Peter Moore fall out of his assumed character far enough to shake his head disgustedly on reading one of these accounts; and my own feelings were fully in accord with his. There is, in my view, no justifiable comparison between the pitting of trapped animals and free sport in the open fields; and I rejoice that in 1911 rat-killing was at long last placed outside the law, along with the similar spectacles—dog-fighting, badger-baiting, cock-fighting—that were declared illegal in the 19th century.

Meanwhile our observations in Barley's parlor continued to be in vain. I could discover no one at all who looked like a particularly close match for John Scott's photograph, and Peter Moore's silence and the continued look of anxiety upon his face assured me that his luck was no better than my own. Yet so large was the room, and so well-filled by men who were constantly coming and going, that neither of us could be sure from moment to moment that our quarry was not close at hand.

Presently I felt a light tug at my sleeve; it came from Murray, who, when I bent down, whispered in my ear: "I seen 'im again, Doctor—'e's in Barley's private office now—that door behint the bar. I seen 'im just now when Barley opened it a bit to send another chap on in."

I nodded, and in a low whisper passed on this intelligence to Moore. A few moments more, and Barley turned over his place behind the bar to an assistant. With a final laughing remark to his friends, the proprietor also retreated into that room.

Moore and I exchanged looks; then, as casually as we could manage it, we both moved into a position from which, when the private door should next be opened, we ought to be able to look into the room beyond. Having accomplished this, I judged that there was nothing for it but to wait, and this we settled down to do.

Soon we could observe a cheerful stir among some men who had gathered near a rear entrance to the parlor. This was occasioned by the appearance of the evening's intended victims. Rats were being carried in, in crates and bags, by the score and by the hundred, to a total that must easily have surpassed a thousand, and the room seemed to fill with their sharp, musky smell. From the entry they were borne across the rear of the parlor, and up a broad stair there. Ample light shone down from a large room or loft above, which seemed to be the scene of the planned entertainment.

Most of the workers engaged in bringing in the rats were young men, and it may have been for this reason that my eye first singled out one older man among them. This was a tall, lean fellow who had a crate upon his shoulder when I first saw him, so that his face was, for the moment, entirely hidden from me; but it was obvious from the long, graying hair that hung uncovered about his ears that he was no longer young. This individual was just starting briskly upstairs with his burden, when my attention was drawn from him suddenly by the reopening of the door of Barley's private office behind the bar. The proprietor himself emerged, leaving the door ajar; but my eager glance toward the room's interior was not as rewarding as I had hoped. I could see part of a desk, a table with a lamp, and three or four battered chairs. In one of these slouched a villainous-looking individual, a complete stranger to me, but who, by reason of his dark hair and hooked nose, could not possibly be the man we sought. The remaining occupant of the room was visible only in the form of a pair of dark-trousered legs, one foot crossed over the other in stylish black boots.

Barley, on coming out into the public room, at once raised his arms and called out in his loud, jovial voice that it was time for the company to move upstairs. Having made this announcement, he retired again into his private chamber and shut the door.

His words brought on a general push in the direction of the stair. Moore and I looked at each other again, and I have no doubt that the disappointment I observed in his face was mirrored in my own.

Yet there was nothing to be gained by losing heart and hope. Barley and the men in the office with him must eventually emerge. Meanwhile, however, if Moore and I were to continue to be inconspicuous, we must go with the crowd. To Murray, who had remained nearby, I imparted this decision with a look and a slight gesture, and by the same means instructed him to remain on watch on the ground floor. With quick intelligence he took my meaning at once.

Then, in the midst of a cheerful throng of men of every class, some carrying dogs, many already wagering for or against particular animals, Moore and I went on up. The room or loft to which we ascended was only a little smaller than that below, and very high, having no ceiling other than the beams of the sloping roof. Despite its spaciousness the air was close; from the crates and bags of rats came an exhalation like that of an open sewer, to mingle with the fumes of tobacco, gin, and beer.

A pit some seven or eight feet square had been constructed in the middle of the floor, by the erection of a thin screen or barrier all round, some two or three feet high, enough to prevent the game from escaping. Ranks of benches, those in the rear somewhat elevated, surrounded the pit, and in it stood a young man with metal clips holding his trousers-legs tight about his ankles, evidently to forestall any desperate rat's effort to seek shelter by that route.

This referee soon called for the first dog scheduled to take part in the evening's competition; its handlers brought it forward, a hundred voices were raised in raucous cries of encouragement or mockery, the wagering became fast and furious, and the sport—if indeed it should be honored with that name—commenced.

It is not my intention to relate in any detail the events taking place in the pit, where time was kept as at a boxing match. Dog succeeded dog, and the total of slain rats mounted rapidly into the hundreds. I recall noticing that Lord Godalming's first terrier did not do well, as one of the intended victims—which were in general remarkable for their apparent helplessness—turned on it and sank sharp teeth into its muzzle. Dr. Seward and its owner withdrew the yelping animal and carried it a little away from the mass of the crowd, endeavoring to do something for its wound.

In my continual scanning of the crowd for any man closely resembling the photograph I had seen of John Scott, I noticed for the second time the tall, ragged rat-carrier. Having evidently completed the labors for which he had been hired, he chose to take no further active part in the proceedings, but sat perched upon a high stool at some little distance from the pit, brooding over the scene and observing with what seemed equal contempt the squealing, growling, panting, bloodied animals and the scarcely less frenzied humans. His wild, graying hair shaded much of his face save for the aquiline nose, and his right hand, propping his head in an attitude of thought, hid much of his mouth and jaw. His countenance was thus suggested to my eyes rather than seen, but I remember that the impression created in my mind by this glimpse was of a visage and a character ravaged and evil, which yet still retained ineradicable evidence of once-great nobility.

Before my attention could become fully focused upon this man, it was drawn away by Peter Moore's touching my arm. We had both declined to join in the rush for seats on the worn benches, and were standing, with others, not far from the head of the stair. This position had the distinct advantage that from it we could look down into the parlor, which was now almost deserted. Near the bottom of the stair young Murray was now standing, looking up, and his eyebrows were excitedly attempting to convey some message to me.

In a moment I understood. Walking toward the foot of the stair from the direction of the bar came Barley and his two confidants; the one who earlier had been visible to me only as trouser-legs and boots was now revealed as a thin young man with a heavy blond mustache.

My eyes of course were fixed at once upon this latter individual, and sought out the tell-tale bulge on the right side of his top hat where a doctor's stethoscope is customarily carried: I rejoiced that during my years of association with Sherlock Holmes I had not failed utterly to develop my powers of observation.

Peter Moore at the same time was leaning close to whisper to me: "That is not John, though there's a strong resemblance." A few seconds, and the three men had ascended the stairs, keeping up a good-humored, low-voiced conversation among themselves meanwhile. Together they passed almost within arm's length of where we stood. The eyes of the villainous-looking one brushed mine; even in this crowd where ruffians were more the rule than the exception, he stood out unpleasantly. His gnarled, wizened frame spoke of advancing age, an impression deepened rather than relieved by his crudely dark-dyed hair. His wrinkled face had an unhealthy, dissipated aspect; but still the firm energy with which he trod the stairs showed him to be not yet decrepit.

The bogus "Scott" almost brushed our sleeves in passing, and I saw him glance at Peter Moore without a trace of recognition. I was just turning over in my mind the rather useless thought that now we wanted Superintendent Marlowe or one of his warehouse clerks to identify the imposter for us, and pondering what we should do without such help, when a disturbance broke out downstairs near the front door. Voices were raised, at first not very loudly but still with an extraordinary tension in them that demanded notice. Murray was signaling again from down below, but in this instance I did not grasp at once the import of his rapid, urgent signs.

Peter Moore was reacting no more rapidly than I, and before either of us had fully grasped the nature of the disturbance, every scoundrel in the throng about us was fully aware of it, and all of them were struggling to reach an exit and escape. The fact was that the uproar in the parlor below had been caused by the entry of a large force of the police.

As I have already remarked, rat-killing was not at that time illegal. Yet it was not unknown for the promoters of these entertainments to add to the bill such contests as badger-baiting, which were already under the prohibition of the law. In such a case those betting on the sport as well as those conducting it would be liable to be charged. Though I had seen no badgers or other animals besides the dogs and luckless rats on Barley's premises, some of the men present must have feared there were, and that they stood in danger of involvement with the wrong end of the law.

Another substantial number must, indeed, have belonged to that class who flee when no man pursueth. The thought that appeared uppermost in nearly every mind was that of escape. A chair was thrown, breaking a window out—but even as I turned at the noise, the head and shoulders of a helmeted policeman appeared framed in the jagged opening. The first-floor exits as well as those on the ground floor had evidently been blocked by Scotland Yard.

Emerging from the melee at the head of the stairs I spied the tall figure of Tobias Gregson. It was only a glimpse I had of Gregson, for my eyes were needed elsewhere. The bogus "Scott," if the man we had spotted was indeed the impostor, was still in my view, and I had no intention of allowing him to escape before he could be questioned.

Peter Moore shared my thought, and side by side we flung ourselves into the pursuit. Though we both put forth our best efforts, however, such was the press of bodies all struggling at cross-purposes that we could make no headway.

We were still near enough to the stair, so that when a woman's scream sounded from that direction and I turned, I could see that it was Sarah Tarlton. She had evidently been foolish or impatient enough to enter the building after all, and was now caught on the stair, between some burly policemen trying to climb, and other men who were attempting to get down. These last were pushed on by still others, behind them, who endeavored to escape. I tried at once to go to her assistance, but soon discovered that whether I strove to move in that direction or the opposite one made very little difference in my actual position.

The entire establishment was by this time in a perfect uproar. As I was spun round almost helplessly in a surging of the crowd, I caught sight once more of the imitation "Scott." He had been one of the first to take alarm, and was now apparently well on the way to making his escape. He had somehow managed to catch hold of one of the overhead beams, which extended completely across the loft some nine or ten feet above the floor, and was in the act of pulling himself up to a standing position on it. Above and beyond him in the shadows, I could see what appeared to be a closed trapdoor or sealed window set in the angle of the roof.

At the next moment I again spied the gray-haired purveyor of rats, just as he leaped with an incredible agility to catch hold of the same beam upon which our quarry balanced. But the ragged, hatless man was prevented from going on by an athletic constable who jumped upward from a chair to catch him by one leg.

The rat-carrier's face was now turned to the full light

of a gas fixture on the wall, and what I saw in that face compelled me instantly to forget all else. A great understanding—as it then seemed—burst upon my brain. An instant later I was hurling men from my path, fighting to reach his side.

But before I could achieve this, a powerful double kick from the dangling man's lean legs sent the body of the athletic constable flying like an acrobat's above the melee. Several men went down beneath the uniformed figure. Once more the ragged man pulled himself up, and once more a policeman would have seized his legs to drag him down; but I was just in time to collar this second officer and pull him, instead, back into the crush. When I let go, the policeman of course glared about, but in the confusion and the press of bodies he was unable to tell who had just foiled him in what he conceived to be the performance of his duty.

When I looked up again, "Scott" had already disappeared—and the ragged man, looking as weightless as a fly, was clambering rapidly toward the closed trapdoor.

Moore had now seized me by the arm, and was shouting as he tugged at me. Following with my eyes the direction of his pointing finger, I could see the villainous-looking fellow who had been with "Scott" and Barley embarking upon a more orthodox climb of his own. He had reached a wooden ladder crudely built against one wall, which evidently furnished the normal means of ascent to the trapdoor and the roof, and around which a throng of men still struggled for the chance to get away.

The crush in general was now thinning out, and the noise diminishing, as men either made good their escapes or, more frequently, fell quiet in the hands of the police. "Dr. Watson!" It was Tobias Gregson at my side. "Is Mr. Holmes here too?"

"No longer," I choked out, meanwhile glancing upward, to where the trap opening now yawned black and empty against the night. "Come this way, and quickly! There is a man who must not escape."

Gregson, shouting to one of his men to join us, came with Moore and me in a rush. Together we made short work of getting through the group of men who were still struggling around the ladder for a chance to climb. Our latest quarry was himself just on the point of being able to get up and away, but, seizing his feet, we dragged him down by main force, despite his desperate struggles to avoid capture.

Gregson and Moore pinioned his arms, and I drew my pistol and presented it to his head, at which point he ceased to struggle.

"Got you, my beauty!" Gregson shouted. "Now where is Dr. John Scott?" And at the same instant I was demanding of the prisoner: "What is your name?"

The wiry form we had surrounded slumped in resignation. "As to Dr. Scott's whereabouts," came the dry answer, "I fear I have been prevented from gaining any useful information. You will oblige me greatly, Watson, by putting up your pistol; my name is Sherlock Holmes."

XI

In his good journeyman style—if not in what I should count as sparkling prose—the late Dr. Watson has provided a substantially correct account of the affair at Barley's upon that long-ago June night. Still there are, to my mind, one or two points where the reader may benefit from a change of viewpoint and a small amount of overlap. Therefore I resume my history at approximately the moment when the police pushed open Barley's front door.

Of course I might have heard them coming from afar, had my attention not been riveted upon that same small private office into which Watson and Moore had been so clumsily attempting to spy. As Watson has noted, my duties as rat-factor had brought me upstairs; but, at the risk of seeming boastful or tedious, let me reiterate for the last time that my hearing is far keener than that of almost any breathing human; so keen that, had the animals and enthusiasts about me been less noisy over their blood sports, I would have had a good chance of understanding almost all that Barley and the other two were saying down in the office, though their voices were quite low.

Their talk was on a subject that lately had begun to grow in fascination for me—rats. One participant of course was Barley—the booming rumble of his voice was unmistakable, however he tried to mute it. The second voice I did not recognize; but the third was indubitably that of my old acquaintance, the still-nameless doctor. I heard it with a throbbing in the needle-marks that scarred my arms—yes, metal can sometimes wound and torture even those it cannot kill.

Regrettably, the hubbub of slaughtered rodents and wounded dogs, and the scarcely more human sounds emitted by the men who watched and wagered, prevented my hearing more than scraps of that distant conversation. And what I could hear of it was damnably oblique and fragmentary, as conversations are wont to be when the subject is a familiar one to all participants and they are arguing technical details. About all I could learn was that the doctor was out to buy several thousand rats as quickly as he could. I thought he expressed some preference for *Rattus rattus;* and it seemed that Barley and the other man were going to act somehow as brokers.

This was not much learned, yet was I content with my situation. I had determined that when my erstwhile oppressor left Barley's, as sooner or later he must, I should not be far behind him; that I should then take the first opportunity to find a place where we would not be interrupted, and speak with him alone; and that in the course of this *tête-à-tête* he would recite to me in a loud, clear voice the names, descriptions, and probable locations of each and every one of his associates in the damnable and mysterious scheme wherein my kidnapping and death were to have been the merest incidents.

The three of course left their real business in the little office, and when they emerged were talking loudly and cheerily about some famed bitch rat-slayer of a past decade. Looking up as he began to climb the stairs, the doctor brushed with his eyes my figure on the high stool, but there was not the faintest hint of recognition in his glance. His mind was no doubt full of things he counted as more important than one dead—as he supposed—old man, however strange. He must have known by then of Frau Grafenstein's demise—the papers had begun to carry the story—but I suppose that like the police he chalked it up to the enterprise of some stray madman, and did not connect it at all with her own efforts in the field of health care. It may have been that any chagrin he felt at the loss of a key employee was offset by relief at the removal of a budding rival.

The three men were just starting up the stair, when the figure of a girl separated itself from a small group near the front of the parlor and came hurrying after them, with the half-furtive manner of someone trying to impart private information. She did not look up in my direction, but I was surprised to recognize the lithe form and scarred face of Sally.

One glance back over her shoulder as the front door came pushing open, and she realized that she was not going to have the time to keep her warning private—she drew in a good breath, and broadcast to the entire establishment the word she had been trying to save for her employer's ears alone:

"Peelers!"

In the next instant her shout was echoed by a score of others. A window crashed, and all was pandemonium, which the good Doctor has already described, although it caught him rather flat-footed when it came.

Whatever the reason for this official exercise by the police, I did not purpose to play a part in it. No more did my enemy the nameless doctor. With a reaction if anything more decisive than my own, he sprang upstairs past Barley—who was stunned to absolute immobility—and had sprinted almost the entire length of the upper room before most of the people in it were aware that anything out of the ordinary was going on. Then from a high bench my foe leaped nimbly for the rafters, into which he swarmed as agile as a sailor.

I had just got myself into motion, calculating to overtake him immediately outside, when there came to my ears a cry of feminine despair, choked and muted but still recognizable as issuing from the throat of Sal. A vital second or two passed before my eyes found her amid the tumult of the crowd below; when I spied her at last she was almost at the front door, unwillingly on her way out in the grip of a sturdy policeman.

For a long moment I was irresolute, which is perhaps the worst possible error when action is required. On the one hand, the strictest demands of honor bound me to Sal's defense. On the other, she was in no grievous peril from the police, whilst across the room my chief known enemy was escaping, a man who would have had Sal killed in an instant had he ever discovered her efforts to set me free.

I turned back to pursue the nimble doctor, but my momentary hesitation had given him a good start, and he was already scrambling along beams high above the dazzle of the hanging lamps, headed straight for a trapdoor in the roof.

Leaping up, I seized a beam myself. Only then did I become aware that policemen, for whatever reason, were converging on me from all directions. Two strong and sweaty arms of the law had me by the leg before I saw them coming, their owner bawling something to the effect that I should now give up peaceably. Whilst I was trying—at first not vigorously enough—to shake him loose, my eyes met those of another man, in civilian clothes, who was rushing toward me, knocking other folk aside. He was of middle size, well built, with something of a bull neck, and a sandy mustache beginning to go gray.

His eyes, expressing shock that demonstrated, as I thought, some recognition, were locked on mine. He cried out, excitedly but in a voice too low for me to understand, a syllable that I took to be a name. Then he sprang forward and astonished me by collaring and dragging back a second policeman, who was about to fasten on me before I had got quite free of the first.

My next kick sent that tenacious officer (from whom the bull-terriers of the pit might have learned something, had they paused to watch) flying above the crowd. This, thanks to my unknown benefactor, ended my direct encounter with the police; however, brief as it was, it had still delayed me long enough for my quarry to get out of the building and out of my sight, slamming the trapdoor shut behind him.

Climbing, I hurled myself at the closed exit, considering direct violence faster than the change of form that would have let me slide out like smoke through the thinnest crevice. But again, a second or two was lost before the bar that my enemy had set in place outside gave way.

Bursting out into the open night at last, I saw that the police, however thoroughly they might have covered the building's first two floors, had been remiss in their planning for the rooftops—or else their men simply had not had time to get into position here before Sal sang out her alarm below. The figure of a lone constable, arms outspread as if to pose for a statue of the guardian law, stood upon a flat neighboring roof some four or five feet distant from Barley's sloping slates. Some thirty feet from the trapdoor, he blocked the single avenue of escape practicable for breathing men. Some ten feet closer to me, his back to me and facing the officer, the blond young doctor crouched, in the act of drawing a revolver from an inner pocket.

At this crucial moment I was once more distracted by an outcry in Sally's voice. This time it was a loud scream, and in such a tone of lost despair that it compelled my immediate allegiance. Behind me as I turned the pistol spoke, the wounded officer cried out, my enemy escaped; but Sal had been tortured for me, and had received my solemn pledge of help, and to my mind my duty was as clear as ever it could be.

Melting at once to bat-shape, I fluttered from the roof down to the police van inside which the last vibrations of that lost scream were dying out. As I recall, there were three vans drawn up in the street, and one, in all propriety, had been reserved for lady prisoners. Alighting on the driver's elevated seat, I resumed human form and at once snatched the reins out of his startled hands. Before he could react he had been pushed off to the ground.

My mental shout was already ringing inside the horses' brains, and they started as if a lion sprang behind them. For several blocks I drove a zigzag course at breakneck pace, scattering traffic from the streets of Soho. Within the lurching van, fresh screams broke out in a wide range of voices; the ladies' coach must have been commandeered from some more prosaic police business and pressed directly into service without a stop to discharge cargo. Over the women's panic I had no control, but I soothed that of the horses, as soon as I was sure we were not being closely pursued, and by degrees reduced their speed, till I could draw them to a halt in a dark mews.

Dropping down behind the van, I tore the padlocks from its door and stood back just in time to escape trampling by a rush of women. From amid this screeching stream, which dissolved into the night in all directions as soon as it emerged, I plucked out Sal. Then, holding one hand clamped over her mouth, I pulled her away with me at a fast trot.

We ran one block and turned a corner, walked quickly for another block and turned again, then walked some more. Sally was quiet now, save for her rapid breathing, and willing to go on with me arm-in-arm. When we had reached an utterly lifeless spot against the outer wall of what I suppose was a factory—by all appearances it might have been a prison—I stopped, and listened. Half a mile or so away, what sounded almost like a small riot was in progress. But still there came no sounds of the chase, and where we were, the night was quiet.

Sal appeared uninjured. "What were they doing to you, girl? Why such a scream?"

"It—it were bein' shut up in that little place. It does me that way sometimes, an' I come all over queer, like I can't breathe."

I sighed, thinking of my lost quarry, lost for no better reason than to relieve this wench from an attack of claustrophobia. But sighs and regrets will gain one neither blood nor honor. I asked: "For what were you arrested, though?"

Sal's breathing, a lonely, frightened sound, had now slowed enough to let her talk easily. "I—I sang out when I saw the peelers at the door. Don't know no other reason.'' There was no recognition in her voice as she scowled toward me through the dark. " 'Ow'd you manage t' get me clean away like that?''

"Do you not know me, Sally?'' I asked, turning my head so that the ghost of light from a far-distant lamp fell on my face.

"I . . . '' She began, and halted. Remember that she had never seen me on my feet before, or in these ragged garments. Remember especially that a full feeding, such as I had enjoyed upon the previous night, will for a time restore to me something of the look of youth. And remember, too, she must have been as certain as were my would-be murderers, that the old man she once had tried to help was dead.

Although my face was no longer a mask of exhausted senility, there was of course a strong resemblance to my debilitated self; so with my voice, though it was now considerably stronger. The truth stood before Sal, struggling to be known; but it was too large and disturbing a truth to be acknowledged at first glance.

"Know you?'' she answered me at last. "Can't say as I do.'' Her voice was high and tense, her last words almost a question.

"As you will, my dear. Why were you at Barley's tonight? Standing sentry for your employers, perhaps?''

"That ain't your business, now, is it?''

"Your welfare has become my business, girl. Was Matthews there as well? I did not see him.''

After a long pause, in which a series of emotions crossed Sal's marred, shadowed face, she shook her head. "Don't know no one by that name.''

"Ah, Sal, trust me.'' I took her patiently by both hands. Though I had lost the doctor, I had Sal now, and so I was in no great hurry. Eventually, through her, the ones I wanted would become accessible. "Did not that old man promise you that there would be no involvement of the police?"

The nervous start in her hands felt to mine like an electric shock. "The old man? Wot old man?"

Gently I patted her right hand into place on my left arm, and off we started walking, a gentleman and his lady. Well, no, it could scarcely have appeared that way. More like, had there been anyone to watch, two of the ragged poor aping the behavior of their betters.

"Now, my dear," I went on, when we had walked half a mile or so, and the tension in the hand upon my arm had started to relax. "Now, you cannot really have forgotten that old man. He'd lost his name, remember? You spoke to him so kindly. And you did more. You very bravely, once, tried to help him—really help. That was shortly before they—took him off."

Her fingers would have pulled free, but could not move. Then slowly, slowly, they were once more persuaded to relax. Her voice, as she murmured "I never 'eard of . . . no old man," faded almost to stunned silence.

I smiled fondly, stroking her captive fingers on my arm, almost as I had soothed the rat. "I'm sure the old fellow never forgot your great kindness. And he did most solemnly promise, no police."

"Sir, don't go a-scarin' a poor girl with talk like that." Had Sal now recognized me, at least on some hidden level of her mind? Her numb voice was sunk so low I had to concentrate to hear it. "If—if yer really wants t' help me, just—just get out o' this and let me go."

"My dear, I might get out o' this, as you put it, at any

time. But I fear that *you* cannot, without help, disentangle yourself from the nets of wickedness. Will you not accept my help?''

''Ah, God . . . .'' We were passing now under a streetlamp, but Sal forgot to try to hide her birthmark as she looked at me with eyes of terror. (How could she fail to know me, now?) ''It'd be as much as me life is worth . . . sir, there's some folk it's death to trifle with.''

''So I have heard.'' I let show in my face the anguish that I sometimes feel, when I am forced to contemplate the evil ways of men. ''I sympathize with your fear.'' Now for a time I only held her hand in silence as we walked, and let her choose the way. ''I'll see you safely home,'' I said.

At the next streetlamp, Sal looked at me very closely once again, this time remembering to use her hair to hide her cheek. She made a small, choked sound, but in this sound there was only a small component of fear, and bolder and bolder grew her eyes probing mine.

Once more the fang-roots in my upper jaw were aching. When we had walked farther still, and I could read unforced consent in Sal's brown eyes, I turned our path into a darker, narrower way, and stopped and pulled her close . . .

It is now common knowledge that the briefest, pleasantest love-making with a vampire will change a breathing human to a fang-sharp monster in a trice. Common knowledge that is of course absurdly wrong. Would you accept the follies of the films and so-called comic books as gospel truth on any other subject? No. To render any man or woman *nosferatu* requires a prolonged exchange of blood; and so when I released

Sal a few blissful minutes later, her throat was marked but her species—as yet—was quite unaltered.

"Now I shall truly see you home," I said. And like a girl who walks and dreams at the same time, Sal put her hand upon my arm and led me promenading down the shabby street.

A drizzle had begun, dissolving the day's dust into slime on the paving stones, before we reached, at the low end of an even meaner street, the hovel she called home. Hers was a cellar room, in a building old even for London, that must have stood sunny in a bird-song field before the city rose like a dirty tide around it.

Sal was reaching with her latchkey for the door at the dark bottom of some stairs, when I put out an arresting hand. In the room beyond the door, a set of lungs—a man's, I thought—was breathing. He might be husband, lover, father—all quite all right with me—but then again he might be something else. When Sal turned up a questioning face to mine, wondering why I held her back, I whispered very softly in her ear: "As soon as you have crossed the threshold, bid me come in."

She looked a question at me still, but unlocked and pushed back the door.

It was deep dark within; though not to my eyes, of course. But Sal started at the scrape of clothing on rough blankets, as the man who had been sprawled upon the room's one cot rose up. One of his great hands swept up from a nearby table a portable electric torch and flashed it in our faces.

"Gorblimey, Sal!" growled out a rough, familiar voice, thick with astonishment. "These ain't no days for bringin' home a trick . . ."

Matthews' voice died as his eyes, widening, fastened upon my face.

Sal ran in to him at once, beginning to babble some apology or explanation, and completely forgetting or ignoring my last words to her. They had not been idle chatter. I, vampire, am unable to enter even the meanest dwelling unless once invited directly to do so.

Her pleading to Matthews did her no more good this time than last. His left hand set down the torch and with easy power seized her hair. He bent her neck, holding her immobile, whilst in his right hand a wicked clasp knife came to be, so smoothly that eyes less experienced than mine might have seen only the flower of the motion, not the growth.

Still wide-eyed, incredulous, he grinned at me but spoke to her. "Now, Sal—yer mean yer don't know who this be?"

"Jem, no! It ain't who you think—the man you think it be is dead."

"Dead! Ar!" It was almost a laugh. "Not 'im! My eyes are workin' fine!"

By now I felt almost as bewildered as the girl. Matthews had never seen me on my feet before, nor with a comparatively youthful face. Beyond doubt he thought he recognized me, but—it dawned upon me rapidly— not as the wretched oldster on the cart. He must know, he must be convinced in his bones as well as in his mind, that that victim was still at the bottom of the Thames. *Then who did he think I was?*

He held the knife now at Sal's throat, and the wonder in his eyes was blending into triumph. His harsh voice rasped at me: "Now let's see just where yer revolver's hid. Tyke off yer coat real slow, and drop it on the floor. Else this gal's done for where she stands—Mr. Great Detective."

XII

"Why, Watson, do you maintain that it was your fault that the man eluded capture?" Sherlock Holmes, in dressing-gown and slippers, put the question to me as he stood before the fire in our sitting room. It was nearly midnight, an hour after the climax of the affair at Barley's. A chill rain had begun to tap upon our windows, and Holmes' hands were spread toward the blaze while he turned his penetrating eyes in my direction. The wrinkles and black hair-dye of his disguise were gone, and he seemed in general none the worse for his desperate struggle to escape Gregson, Moore, and myself. Yet I did not much care for his pale, finely drawn appearance.

"Why should it have been your fault?" Holmes repeated. "I understand that the suspected killer had already made good his escape before you chose me as your quarry. And even if you had not stopped me, I would not have caught him—I must admit that I was in pursuit of other game myself."

I took a chair beside the fire, and tasted the brandy he had just poured for me. "Holmes, I saw no point in confessing to the police that it was I who collared one of their men, and thus deliberately gave the murderer his chance to get free. But I must confess it now."

Holmes sat down across from me. "You collared a

policeman?'' His voice sounded too tired to express the full surprise that he must naturally have felt. "My dear old fellow—why?''

"It is very simple. Because I did not know the man escaping was the maniac whom the police had launched the raid to capture. I was convinced that the man escaping was yourself.''

Holmes leaned back in his chair, and there was a long pause before he spoke. "He looked like me, then. Very much like me.'' The words were quiet, with a fatalistic lack of emotion in them.

Peering anxiously at my friend's haggard features, I went on: "With the first good look I got at the fellow's face, I recognized—there is no other way to put it—I recognized it as yours. The same aquiline nose, the same strong chin and piercing eyes. Yes, even the same figure, tall and lean and very active.''

"The very same. I see,'' Holmes echoed in that doomed voice.

"Oh, there were some differences, I admit.'' I frowned at my friend's uncharacteristically passive acceptance of this news. "I think he was an older man than you. His hair was longer and grayer, and his eyebrows bushy. His color was less healthy.'' Although, even as I was speaking, I thought that there was no longer much difference of complexion.

"You heard him speak?''

"No.''

"Go on.''

"There is little more to tell. I am well acquainted, of course, with your skill at disguise, and it struck me as perfectly natural that you should have altered your appearance before visiting a place like Barley's, where some enemy might otherwise recognize you.''

Holmes' eyes glittered. "Did it not then seem strange that you could recognize me at once?"

"Perhaps," I went on, somewhat wounded by this petulance, "you do not believe the resemblance was as strong as I have painted it?"*

"My dear fellow," he muttered, "excess imagination is not your great fault. Yes, Watson, I believe you. I only wish that I did not . . . but go on."

I did not know what else to say, and with a gesture tried to convey as much. Then we were both silent for a time. A coal falling in the grate made what seemed a loud, intrusive noise. Holmes' gaze had turned in that direction, introspectively, and the look of his face now made me fear a return of his illness of the early spring.

"Yes, I believe you," he repeated at length. "And it is no blame to you that the fellow got away. If we are to assign blame for that, we must charge the Fates, or Fortune . . . but what good ever comes of that? You were quite right, too, not to speak of the incident to Lestrade or the others."

"You did not see this man at Barley's yourself, Holmes?"

"I?" He roused himself, as if surprised to find me still in the room. "No, not to my knowledge, save for a fleeting glimpse of his ragged back. I had never thought that Fate would send the waterfront killer there . . . but the identification seems well-founded. I am told that Jones—as Lestrade's latest pet informer calls himself—is completely positive that the man whose presence at Barley's he reported is the same who was with him at the hostel, and there broke down the doors.

---

*Readers who doubt the strength of this similarity would do well to re-read the descriptions of Holmes and myself set down by our contemporary chroniclers in the 1890s.—D.

I mean to speak to Jones tomorrow, and form my own estimate of his reliability. Meanwhile . . .''

Holmes sighed sharply. With an air of casting intro-spection to the winds, he raised his hands and clapped them down decisively on the chair arms. ''Watson.''

''Yes?''

''What do you know of vampires?''

''Vampires? Some species of tropical bats.''

''Good old Watson! I am speaking of vampirism in human beings.''

I was chilled by my friend's apparent seriousness. ''Walking corpses? Of course it is all pure—rubbish.'' I had been about to say, pure lunacy; but with that pale, tormented, utterly intent face before me, I found myself suddenly unable to use the word.

''Not corpses, Watson.'' Holmes studied me care-fully. Then his manner became—deliberately, as I thought—more casual. ''It is in the realm of legend, of course. But think of it nevertheless. You will do that much if I ask it, will you not?''

''Certainly, but . . .'' Again, I did not know how to continue. The silence this time stretched on until I, at least, felt it grow painful, and was constrained to speak. ''Lestrade said that the fellow killed again.''

''Meaning the constable killed on the roof.'' Holmes stood up and stretched, an action reassuringly normal. ''Join me, Watson? I perceive a cold partridge upon the sideboard, and a bottle of Montrachet. Have I told you that I now know the name of the man impersonating Scott? It is David Fitzroy—a thoroughly bad man, and a clever one. He is a doctor himself—I think you have heard me say before that when a doctor does go bad, he has the nerve and the knowledge to make him the worst of criminals. I should not be at all surprised to find a medical man at the very bottom of this evil tangle.''

"But not, in this case, a killer.''

"In that I think you and Lestrade are wrong. The constable was shot, remember. Fitzroy fled through the trapdoor to the roof just ahead of the man from the docks, and I rather doubt whether my look-alike was carrying firearms, or would have used them.''

"Why on earth not, seeing that he killed so savagely before?''.

Again Holmes bestowed a long, speculative look upon me before he answered. ''I think you may take my word for it, that pistols would not be consistent with his— peculiar madness.''

I did not understand, but neither did I wish to concentrate my friend's attention any further upon that individual whose exploits seemed to disturb him so. ''Are the two men somehow in league, then? I wonder what the connection can be between them?''

We were at the sideboard now, and Holmes poured each of us a glass of wine. "For one thing, Watson: rats. Fitzroy wanted—I think he wanted desperately, for some reason—to purchase a thousand or more of them, and soon. He said he intended using them in some kind of show, similar to Barley's—all purely a blind, of course, though in my guise as fellow entrepreneur I pretended to believe him, and expressed a wish to sell him some.''

Holmes moved to take down the Medical Directory from my shelf, and opened it. ''Aha. We see here, that as late as two years ago, Dr. David Fitzroy was one of the young physicians working with Sir Jasper Meek himself, in precisely the same field of research as that which sent John Scott off to Sumatra. Fitzroy has accompanied Sir Jasper on at least one expedition to that area."

"The connections grow, then."

"They do indeed."

I picked at the food upon my plate. "Is it possible, I wonder, that Lestrade is right? That the madman who killed Frau Grafenstein is Dr. Fitzroy's escaped patient?"

Holmes, I was glad to see, was attacking his own food with determination if not actually relish. He did not answer me directly, but asked: "Have you ever wondered, Watson, just what the lady was doing in such a place at midnight?"

"I have wondered, but could think of no good reason for her presence."

"You should endeavor, then, to think of a possible bad one. According to my informants, the Grafenstein woman was considered, some ten years ago, to be one of the most brilliant young biologists on the Continent. She was forced to resign her university position, under a cloud whose exact nature I have as yet been unable to discover, but which seems to have had some substance. I have as yet no clue as to just what she was doing here in London—aha."

As he spoke, Holmes had moved near the window. The drizzle continued, with fog, and traffic was light in Baker Street. At such a late hour, it was evident that only business of some terrible urgency could bring us visitors. Yet, as I saw when I moved closer to the window myself, an unmarked carriage had certainly just stopped before our door.

Mindful of earlier days when assassins had watched

us from below, I moved to draw Holmes farther from the window. He allowed himself to be turned away. But at the same time remarked in a tired voice: "I don't think these visitors have come to shoot at me, old fellow. If my conjecture regarding their purpose is correct, they mean us no harm; but still I ask very earnestly that you do not retire just yet."

"Of course. But whatever they want, you had better send them away; we are both of us already exhausted."

"I shall, if such a course is possible. I fear it may not be." With these words, Holmes seemed to shake off in a moment all his fatigue and dullness. With the air of a man plunging into cold water, he went out our door and down the stairs, so quickly and lightly that when he pulled open the street door he surprised a distinguished-looking old gentleman in the very act of reaching for the bell. Another man, younger and even more elegantly attired, stood beside the first visitor on the steps, and both gazed with some amazement at our two dressing-gowned figures that had so suddenly appeared.

"Come in, gentlemen, come in," Holmes invited, his tone completely business-like. New energies had been mobilized from somewhere in his great reserves, and he might just have risen from a refreshing sleep.

One of the men who now ascended to our rooms was Sir Jasper Meek himself, the elderly and very eminent physician whose name had come up in our talk only minutes before. However striking this coincidence might have seemed ordinarily, at the time it was all but lost upon me, in the great wonder that I felt upon recognizing our second visitor. Although I am writing for posterity and not for immediate publication, I fear that prudence prohibits my naming him, or even describing his person in any detail. Nor shall I recount the first introductory remarks that passed among us.

Suffice it to say, that when we were all of us settled round a replenished fire, this younger of our visitors wasted not a moment in getting down to business. "Mr. Holmes, I need not tell you that only a matter of an importance impossible to exaggerate has brought us to your door, without notice and at this late hour."

"No, you need not tell me that," Holmes answered quietly. "Pray continue. You may speak as freely before Dr. Watson as before me."

"Very well. It is a crime of attempted blackmail with which we are concerned."

"I am not surprised."

"Not blackmail such as you must have dealt with in the past, Mr. Holmes. No affair of the heart. And this case is not confined to any single personage, however—eminent." The speaker gestured with a practiced flourish. "This great city about us, the heart of empire, is itself being held for ransom."

I actually sprang to my feet with an exclamation, but the effect upon Holmes was nothing like so strong. His gray eyes had taken on a hard, penetrating stare, but he merely nodded, as if receiving confirmation of an idea already held in private.

The two men on our settee exchanged glances. "You will understand, Mr. Holmes, and you, Dr. Watson," the speaker continued, "why no public announcement of the peril has yet been made, and why in fact none is contemplated. Even the official police have not been notified, though our full appreciation of the danger is now some hours old. The city is bursting with visitors from every corner of the Empire, nay, of the world, come to do Her Majesty honor. Any mass panic under these conditions would . . . '' Here our exalted visitor had to pause, to try to master his emotions.

Sir Jasper Meek cleared his throat, and passed a hand over his high, pale forehead, so in contrast with the tanned parchment of his cheeks. ''Gentlemen, the thing is this. There have already been several cases in the metropolis of London . . . of a most contagious and most terrible disease.'' Now he, too, hesitated.

''These cases you mention,'' Holmes snapped, ''are of course meant as proof of the blackmailers' power to accomplish what they threaten, which is to loose an epidemic among us. And the disease is plague. Well, how much do the villains demand, and how and where is it to be delivered?''

Had Holmes presented a revolver and ordered our visitors to hand over their purses, their astonishment could scarcely have been greater. Both of them, faces frozen, stared at him in silence for the space of several breaths. Then the man I have not named pulled from a pocket a small piece of paper, which he handed over to Holmes. My friend took it eagerly. Looking over his shoulder, I read part of the note, which had been composed by pasting onto a sheet of white paper printed letters and words evidently clipped from one or more newspapers. The closing words of the message were:

UNLESS OUR DEMANDS ARE GRANTED, GOD SAVE THE QUEEN INDEED AND THE EMPIRE TOO. LET THERE BE NO TRICK-ERY OR A MILLION WILL DIE AS THIS MAN DIED.

The speaker continued, in a voice that came near

breaking: "No instructions have as yet been given us for the delivery of the ransom. But what is demanded—in an earlier note, that we at first dismissed as the work of a mere crank—is nothing less than a million pounds."

I burst out again with some exclamation, at which, I think, no one bothered to look up. Our eminent visitor went on: "The note you hold, Mr. Holmes, was found pinned to the garment of the third and latest victim, an elderly man still unidentified. His body was dropped from a vehicle of some sort, earlier this evening, directly in front of the house of Sir Jasper in Harley Street. Sir Jasper had earlier received a message warning him to expect something of the sort."

"Have you that note, too? Excellent! Thank you." Holmes held the two papers for a moment to the light. Then he asked: "The victim was, I suppose, dressed in a peculiar kind of hospital shirt or gown, the sleeves held on by small cloth ties?"

If our visitors had been stunned by Holmes' earlier remark, this question cast them into a state approaching paralysis. At last they stammered out some confirmation; and from a small bag which he had been carrying, Sir Jasper now produced a garment which, when unrolled, looked like the twin of the shirt discovered on the pier.

"Gentlemen," he advised us, "I have treated this with carbolic, as was necessary to eliminate the danger of contagion. Otherwise it is just as I myself removed it from the latest plague victim's body."

Holmes accepted the garment and held it up, spread out.

"I see no bullet-holes," I remarked, no doubt rather thoughtlessly, in my excitement.

Sir Jasper gave me a peculiar glance. "We have said, Dr. Watson, that the man died of plague."

With a quick half-smile in my direction, Holmes bent to open a lower drawer of his desk. From the drawer he took out another roll of cloth, and spread it out upon his desk beside the first. The bewilderment in our visitors' faces could scarcely be said to increase, but their expressions seemed to acquire a frozen permanence as they beheld the two shirts side by side.

"Two things I must assure you of, gentlemen," Holmes' voice crackled now, and he smiled no more. "The first is that the threat you have received is in the most deadly earnest; and the second is that there is a good chance of its being carried out."

XIII

I can only describe the pressure that kept me from entering Sal's apartment by comparing it with the force that would prevent either breathing man or vampire from leaping in a single bound to the top of a hundred-story building; just so impossible was it for me to move a centimeter past the threshold without invitation.

"The coat!" Matthews rasped at me again, from across the squalid room. "Just tyke it off now, real easy-like." The knife in his hand prodded with precise calculation at the girl's soft throat, where one small bright drop of blood appeared.

My own right hand, extended at shoulder height, was hidden from his view behind the frame of the doorway in which I stood. It had gone to work with all its strength on the old masonry that mouldered there. Tired mortar crunched and cracked beneath my rage-driven talons, and a fist-sized stone was loosening.

To cover the sounds made by my busy fingers, and to try to gain time for them to complete their work, I endeavored to draw my enemy into an argument. As he obviously took me for some detective or other, I played the role: "Think what you are doing, Matthews. This is not a killing matter—not yet. Put down the knife, release the girl, and you shall never stand in the dock for any crime you may have committed so far. You have my solemn word on that."

Matthews had no intention of believing me, or even of listening. "Your coat, I said! Or, by God, I'll carve 'er!"

My straining fingers at last pulled the stone out of the wall. Time was when my right hand knew cunning with spear and lance and javelin. I twisted my body and threw with all the force that I could muster. The hurled stone cracked Matthews' wrist, jarring the blade out of his hand—but from there the stone glanced on in a way that I had not foreseen, to smash into his forehead. He fell without a groan, to hit the floor almost before his clashing weapon.

Sal cried out, and she too went down, although the blade had left only the merest scratch upon her throat. For a long moment there was stark silence in the cellar, save for her solitary, gasping breath, and the uneven thumping of her heart. Then she raised her head, grasping the fact that the deadly peril of the knife had somehow been averted. She jumped up, hysterical though still almost silent, and would have run past me to the street.

I caught her gently in the doorway. "Sally, you must invite me in. Bid me come into your dwelling, dear. Sally—?"

It took a minute to extract from her the coherent words I needed. With their pronouncing, the overwhelming resistance to my entry was gone at once. (It could have been only psychological, you say? But so is life.) Now I could walk her to a chair, where I settled her and soothed her, and kissed the thrice-marred whiteness of her throat. Leaving her still quietly a-tremble, I walked over to the far wall, to see if a source of information might be salvaged.

Alas, it was at once apparent that no sort of appeal—even from me—was going to make much impression upon my quondam opponent. His eyes were half open and his vital signs had all but disappeared. Where the stone had struck his forehead there was a visible depression. Cursing my ill-fortune, I let him fall back to the floor.

At this, Sal let out a faint shriek, and I turned to regard her thoughtfully. Tremoring and twitching, staring now into space, she was seemingly indifferent even to the full display of her great birthmark in the reflected harshness of the electric lantern which still glowed where Matthews had left it on the table. I sighed. It was becoming plain to me, however belatedly, that Sal's good-hearted nature was very ill-suited to stresses of the kind that Fortune had lately visited upon her. The very gentleness and sensibility which could not bear to see a sick old man disposed of in the Thames, now began to appear as possible liabilities to that old man's cause.

Ah, Sal! If only, before Jem Matthews, there had come into your life some solid London workman, with love that could be blind to your marked face—but of course at seventeen she had had very little time for such a miracle.

I stood before her and patiently held out my hand, until hers came to take it. She shuddered at the contact now. Her face began to turn away, but stopped because her gaze had locked itself almost unwillingly on mine. There were the two little raw punctures on her throat. They would be extremely slow to heal; but heal they would, if we embraced no more, and with their disap-

pearance all signs and shadows of my vampire presence
would vanish from her mind and body.

Now softly I entreated her. "My dear? Dear Sal?"
And when at length I saw enough awareness in her eyes
I went on: "We must now consider how best to keep
you safe. If any of Matthews' associates observe you in
this state, they are sure to consider you dangerously
unreliable. And should they connect you even indirectly with his death—well, you would not be safe at
all. I can of course remove his body from your dwelling, but—"

Terror had been slowly replacing the blankness in
her face. "It *was* you on that bloody cart." She made it
an accusation. "In irons, lookin' like an old 'un—I
seen you there." Her voice fell to an awed whisper. "I
know they drowned you—didn't they? Or was it
smothered? *Yer a dead 'un now.*"

I shook her—oh, just a little, very gently—and persisted. "Never mind about all that—about the old man.
The question now is, what is to be done with you?"

Sal's gaze had turned toward the still form huddled
by the wall. "He was my man—my Jem. You killed
'im . . . broke 'is neck like a chicken . . . like a
bloody rat . . ."

Now this was neither accurate nor apposite, to say
nothing of the lack of gratitude it showed. I resumed my
shaking of the wench, this time with a little briskness of
irritation. Still there was no restorative effect, and I
soon let her go.

I paced around the wretched room, came back. "My
own thought, my dear," I said, "is that you had best be
taken straight to the police. They can protect you both
day and night, as long as those who work with Matthews are still alive. Are you presently wanted by the

police? For anything, I mean, besides giving the alarm at Barley's?''

Sal continued to stare at the body of the one she thought of—now, at least—as "her man." She did not answer me at all.

Oh, I might have brought her out of it, even restored her to a temporary gaiety. There are ways. But those ways would not have been good for her in the long run. And the danger to her from her criminal associates would have remained.

"Come! Answer!"

She turned to face me, and swallowed. "No—no, the peelers don't want t' buckle me, 'cept fer wot I did at Barley's.''

"Then to the peelers, as you call them, you shall go. And you must tell them all you can—be willing to give evidence and they'll protect you day and night. Tell them where that building is, where I was held a prisoner. And say you'll testify against that young doctor—what's his name?''

"Dr. David Fitzroy. I 'eard it once.''

"Fitzroy." I breathed the name a few times, savoring its syllables. "And also any of the others whom they can manage to arrest. Name them all. Fitzroy is the leader?''

"Not 'im. The way 'e talked sometimes, I know 'e got 'is orders that 'e 'ad t' follow.''

"From?''

"I dunno who." A ghost of Sal's normal spirit showed in her eyes, and glad I was to see it. "Me turn evidence? Stand up t' peach on 'em in court? Ah, if I on'y dared! Jem'd be alive now if it weren't fer them.''

"You must dare. Never fear, you will not be called

upon to testify, as they shall never come to trial. I swear it, as I swore the same to Matthews.''

"Ah . . .''

"Fitzroy." Once more I enjoyed the name. "Yes, you must tell the peelers all you can, even about me, I shall not mind. And they will keep you safe—for long enough.''

"Ah . . .''

"But all you mean to tell them, you must tell me first. . . .''

XIV

Late though the hour was, and tired as we all were, the urgency of the matter would not allow of any delay. Holmes and I dressed, went down with our visitors to the waiting carriage, and rode with them at a brisk pace through almost deserted streets. Then, at the same hospital where I had first encountered Sherlock Holmes, in a small, guarded dissecting-room not far from that very laboratory, Sir Jasper Meek showed us the body which had been so horribly deposited before his door.

The corpse was that of a grizzled and unshaven man, past middle age, and thin as any of the homeless poor. It bore the classical tokens of the plague, in the form of hard, black swellings in groin and armpits. Additional marks on wrists and ankles indicated that the victim must have been heavily manacled at, or shortly before, the time of his death.

Holmes, bending close through the reek of carbolic to examine the body, soon disposed of our impression that the man had been a derelict in life.

"The illiterate poor," said he, "do not spend a great deal of time holding a pen between thumb and forefinger, as this man undoubtedly did. We might bring in the next of kin of any elderly clerks reported missing during the last month or six weeks. It may help us if we can learn this victim's identity, and how and when he was taken as an experimental subject—are our opponents seizing people on the street at random for that purpose?"

"The police, then, are to be notified?"

"I recommend informing Inspector Lestrade, after swearing him to secrecy. He has the capacity to follow instructions to the letter—once he can be made to understand them—and also to keep a closed mouth when necessary. Yet we must not tell even Lestrade the full story. Not yet."

Holmes returned to his examination of the corpse. "These small red marks clustered on the chest—they have the appearance of flea-bites, have they not, Sir Jasper?"

"Indeed they have," replied the illustrious physician. "Though why they should be so curiously concentrated I cannot guess. The body elsewhere is remarkably free of any evidence of attack by vermin. I say remarkably, assuming this man to have been kept in poor and unhealthy conditions during the last days of his life."

"Quite. Well, unhealthy is surely not too strong a word."

I ought perhaps to interject a comment here, to avoid puzzling my future readers unnecessarily. It was not until 1905, some eight years after the events herein described, that the bite of fleas was generally understood by the medical community to be the ordinary means of transmission of plague to humans—although as early as 1894 it had been confirmed by repeated studies that epidemics of plague in rats coincided closely with those in man. John Scott's work in

Sumatra, had any of his results survived, might have greatly speeded the advance of science in this direction.

In 1894, also, Alexandre Yersin in Hong Kong, and Kitasato in Japan, both succeeded independently in isolating the plague bacillus, *Pasteurella pestis;* and in the following year Yersin had prepared a serum to combat the disease. Recalling this as I stood in the dissecting-room, I mentioned the existence of a serum to Sir Jasper, but he only looked grave and shook his head. Of course, months of effort would have been necessary to provide London with enough of the serum to be of substantial help against an epidemic.

The door opened, and a senior official of the hospital, his face very grave, looked in to make an announcement. "Gentlemen, more police are here with another body that has just been found. The marks appear similar."

Holmes at once directed that this cadaver also be brought into our room, where it was laid out upon the remaining table. I was scarcely surprised to hear that this corpse had been brought up during the continued dragging of the Thames near the murder site. When found, it had been sealed inside one of John Scott's oilcloth bags, and wearing one of the peculiar shirts that had made up part of his expedition's equipment. The body had been in the water too long—perhaps a month, I judged—for us to be able to determine whether there were any flea-bites on the chest.

Working beside me in the intolerably close, foul air, Holmes suddenly swayed, so that I felt it necessary to put out an arm and steady him. He muttered to me in a low whisper: "But I feel sure that the fleas bit this man also, Watson. Again, the drinking of the blood. Do you see? The fleas will have it, or the other. And in this case which is deadlier?''

I tightened my grip upon his arm. "Holmes, you are coming home with me. Immediately, for you must rest.''

For once, I think, I was as forceful as he himself was wont to be. Still, when he acquiesced almost meekly, I was surprised. Holmes perhaps enjoyed my reaction, for there was a faint twinkle in his eyes when we had taken leave of the others and were out of the dissecting-room. "As yet, Watson, no directions have been given for the delivery of the ransom. Do you mark that? It means that we have yet a little time to spare. It may mean that things do not go smoothly for the blackmailers. I pray that it is so . . . but in any case, you are right, now is the time to rest.''

Early next morning, Lestrade appeared at Baker Street. The inspector was somewhat mystified by the orders he had received from his superiors to cease work on all his current cases and place himself completely at Holmes' disposal. He came in bemoaning the fact that he was thus being forced, without explanation, to drop his work on the Grafenstein killing. And this just when, as he put it, there had been "a shocking development, but one that promised to be helpful.''

"And what might that be?'' Holmes demanded sharply.

"Why, another murder.''

Lestrade went on to inform us that one Jem Matthews, formerly of "the fancy,'' and since his retirement from the ring one of the most accomplished ruffians in London, had been brutally slain during the night just past, in the lodgings of a young woman named Sally Craddock. "You might have noticed her at Barley's, gentlemen. She was the one who gave the alarm. And she had just been arrested and put into the van there when that scoundrel we were after leaped onto it somehow and drove off."

Lestrade went on to explain that an hour or so before dawn the girl had walked into the Commercial Street police station, of her own volition and evidently in a state of shock, to report Matthews' killing. She had begun to give evidence, saying that the wanted man—whose name she insisted she did not know—had quarreled with Matthews, and had slain him somehow by brute strength when Matthews drew a knife. Then, in the midst of being questioned, Sally Craddock had fallen into a deep sleep of exhaustion, almost a coma; a police surgeon was in attendance upon her now.

I was glad that Holmes and I had had the chance for a few hours' sleep and some breakfast, for within minutes of Lestrade's arrival the two of us were in a cab and once more on our way to the East End, while the inspector at Holmes' orders had begun his search for information regarding missing clerks.

"You are certain, then," I asked Holmes as we rode, "that Jem Matthews' killing is connected somehow with the blackmail scheme?"

"If it was in fact done by the same man, the one we have been searching for. And there seems little doubt of that."

"This mad fellow appears to be at the center of it all."

"He is at the center, certainly, or very near it. But I think he is not mad. Watson, we were interrupted last night just as I was trying to reconstruct the events taking place on the pier and culminating in the Grafenstein woman's death.''

"I am prepared to listen.''

"But you do not yet, I think, see the importance of these events in the whole tangled skein of crime confronting us. In this I include not only the violent deeds of this peculiar killer, but the blackmail threat, and even the disappearance of John Scott.''

"I am also prepared to learn.''

"Excellent. Let us then begin with Frau Grafenstein standing or walking on the dock at approximately midnight, her pistol in her purse and, I fear, no very good intentions in her heart.''

I interrupted: "How do you know she was not brought to that deserted spot against her will?''

"By some assailant who allowed her to retain her pistol? Whom, nevertheless, she did not attempt to resist until that lonely place was reached? It is conceivable, I suppose—but let us try another hypothesis first.''

"Yes, I see. Go on, Holmes.''

"As I remarked to Lestrade, the river is very often used to dispose of bodies. We saw last night evidence that it has been so used, for a month or longer, by those who are now threatening to loose the plague upon us. Surely it needs no very great leap of the imagination to suppose that Frau Grafenstein, given her background in chemical science and its abuses, was in league with them. That her presence on the dock was connected with the disposal of yet another experimental victim. But this time—something went wrong.''

Holmes' eyes turned piercingly upon me as he went on. "At some hour near midnight, her short-barreled but powerful pistol was fired; at or about the same time, matching bullet-holes were made in the shirt, and a bullet of a caliber to fit the pistol lodged in the boathouse wall. Also, the lady had her throat torn out.

"Again concurrently, or nearly so, the oilcloth bag containing the manacles was left in the water near the spot. Does it suggest anything to you, Watson, that when that sealed bag was recovered it contained no body? And no shirt, whereas we found a wet shirt on the pier?"

I replied: "The intended victim was not dead after all, and managed to escape."

"Very good! I do not mean to imply that your answer is the wrong one, when I repeat that the bag when found was still fastened shut, not cut or torn in any way. I wish only to point out what a very remarkable escape that must have been."

Another thought, somewhat distracting, had just occurred to me. "Holmes, if what you say is true, this man is most probably infected with the plague. If it should go into the pneumonic form, he will represent a deadly peril to the whole city, with every breath he takes."

My friend was silent for a moment, and I thought he looked at me strangely. "I cannot say it is impossible, Watson. But I think that particular danger is not one which need greatly concern us."

"I am sure I do not see why, if this man is infected."

Holmes peered ahead, impatient at some snarl of traffic that was momentarily delaying us. "Do you recall, Watson, those scratches on the planking of the dock? I examined them very carefully."

"I do."

"The radius of their arcs was equal to the length of

long human arms—of arms as long as mine—or of the arms of the man who wore that shirt."

There came an unfamiliar creeping sensation along my scalp. There seemed to loom, just beyond the limits of my understanding and imagination, some horror that threatened to unnerve even Sherlock Holmes, and which he was endeavoring to point out to me—to point out slowly and indirectly, as if he were reluctant to speak of it at all. For the first time in my life, perhaps, I truly understood how a vague danger may sometimes be more terrible than one definitely known. "Holmes," I cried, "I do not see what you are getting at."

His eyes again were fixed on mine relentlessly. "Those scratches were made by the killer, Watson. By the same man, tall, lean, inhumanly strong, who so closely resembles me—and who has now killed again. My one hope, Watson, my one hope is . . ."

"Yes?"

"That he is killing with justification. In self-defense or with some other purpose that he considers honorable."

I thought aloud: "He stole money from the woman's purse."

"He took her money, yes. But he might have seen that as an honorable act—to the victor belong the spoils of war. I have hopes, because he next scrupulously *bought* the clothing that he needed."

"A peculiar concept of honor, I should say. For a man of this day and age, at any rate."

As if to himself, Holmes murmured: "Ah, if I could only be sure *that he is not*."

"I fail to understand."

He shook his head. "I spoke of my one hope. If he is

behaving honorably, that means he is actually our ally, an ally we sorely need against our terrible enemies—and he may gain for us the time we need."

"His feats are certainly incredible."

"No ordinary human being could match them." Holmes sounded now like a professor encouraging a student, and he was still watching me intently.

Not knowing what I was expected to say, I went on: "He is a madman, certainly, and in his paroxysms must be immensely ferocious and strong. But we have known that from the first."

Holmes said evenly: "I think he is not a madman. It is my belief that this man is a vampire."

For a time there was no sound in our cab but that of its creaking motion, and the steady beat of the horse's hooves. A kind of mist had come before my eyes, and I could find no words with which to reply.

My friend's voice now seemed to reach my ears from a great distance. "Watson, I know it is a hard thing when the mental habits of a lifetime must be discarded. Had I not—had I not some private sources of information, I might well be as reluctant as you are to face the truth. But I shall need your help when I stand face to face with this vampire, and nothing less than the truth will serve to prepare you for the confrontation."

What was I to do? In my despair I realized that to suggest to Holmes that he was not himself, that overwork had at last taken its toll upon his mind, would be worse than useless. The least harmful result I could imagine was that he would no longer communicate his true thoughts to me at all—and that, I felt, would prevent my helping him in any way toward recovery.

Meanwhile Holmes' voice pursued me, and in it I now heard the dreadful certainty of madness. "Think,

Watson: the man survived not only infection with the plague, but drowning, and after that a gunshot through the body. Think of the horrible strength and ferocity that tore out the woman's throat and took her blood, then pulled apart those iron locks and heavy timbers at the hostel. No doubt we shall see fresh evidence of the same powers at the end of this little ride."

"I must think about it, Holmes. You must give me time to grasp it."

"Of course." I could hear a certain weary relief in my friend's voice. He thought that I was almost ready, or at least on the way to being ready, to grant that he was right. I had deceived my friend. My heart sank further, if that were possible.

"And now," he added, "here we are."

It was a vile neighborhood in which our cab had stopped. Here, as at the docks, I glimpsed the little mob of curious onlookers kept at a distance by police; here again, there stood a uniformed officer on guard, this time at a dark doorway, into which he passed us with a nod.

Having groped our way down into the damp and dimness of a wretched cellar apartment, we found To- bias Gregson, his electric torch in hand, evidently mak- ing an inch-by-inch search of the floor for clues. At our arrival he scrambled to his feet and offered greetings, his face a study in mixed emotions.

Holmes now seemed almost buoyant. "Have you any word yet, Gregson, on the identity of your sup- posed maniac?"

"No sir, we have not. It's my own thinking now that he's not escaped from anyone's custody, but has just freshly gone off his nut."

"Well, this latest modification of the official theory

has the attractive quality of some freshness, at any rate. Now let us inspect the evidence."

A second electric torch was resting on a small, shaky table; Holmes picked it up and tried it. "Switched on, you see, Watson, but the batteries are dead. Gregson, if I might borrow yours for a moment? Thank you. And so, here is the killer's latest victim."

Against the far wall of the cellar lay the body of a man dressed in cheap clothing. Though he was young and powerfully built, in death his brutal features had acquired a curiously aged, exhausted look. In the middle of the forehead a great depressed fracture was plainly visible, beneath a discoloration of the skin.

Holmes ignored this for the moment and examined the throat particularly. "No sign of a wound here. Do you think, Watson, this man has been exsanguinated?"

"I think not."

"Gregson, what did the medical examiner say?"

"Sir?"

"The question is, has this body been drained of blood?"

Gregson blinked. "No sir, nothing was said along that line."

Beside the man's body lay an evil-looking clasp-knife, open. This Holmes now picked up, and on the tip of its blade he declared a tiny bloodstain to be visible.

Gregson commented: "That'll support the girl's story, Mr. Holmes. I mean that this beauty here was threatening her."

"I am very anxious to speak with her; but still I felt it necessary to look in here first. Right wrist broken, wouldn't you say, Watson?" Holmes was offering me the dead man's arm to feel, as impersonally as if it had been a chicken wing.

Taking the lifeless, heavily-muscled limb into my grasp, I found I could make the bone-ends grate against each other beneath the skin. "Yes. Also, there seems to be no doubt about the cause of death." I pointed to the ruined forehead.

"And very little doubt, that it was done with this." Holmes picked up a fist-sized stone also lying nearby. "A good match with those in the walls. And observe the bits of mortar still adhering to it." He shone the torch about into the room's dim corners. "The electric light may prove to be one of the most practical aids to the criminal investigator since the invention of the microscope. . . . But where did this piece come from?"

Holmes had to go out into the stairwell with the light before his search was successful. "Here, at about shoulder level. And the stone was dug out very roughly; with the fingers, it would appear."

The face of Gregson, looking over Holmes' shoulder, took on an injured expression. "No need to pull our legs, sir. Walls here may not be solid as a cathedral, but to remove that piece still took a bit o' work with steel tools, I fancy."

Holmes fitted the stone into the hole, where it matched fairly neatly. Some mortar was missing, which could be seen in the form of dust and scattered small pieces at our feet. With a sigh my friend snapped off the torch and returned it to its owner. "No doubt it is as you say, Gregson. Come along then, Watson; I look forward very eagerly to a talk with Miss Sally Craddock."

In a few minutes we were at the Commercial Street police station, where Holmes was of course well known by the authorities. We were shown at once to the small room in which the girl was being temporarily held. As the door opened, I saw her seated, in conversation with a matron; and although her face was turned partially away, I recognized her at once as the young woman whose great strawberry birthmark I had remarked at Barley's.

Her appearance as we entered, and the vivacity with which she turned her head to see who we were, showed that she was much recovered from the dazed condition in which Lestrade had reported her to be. Holmes at once stepped forward, saying: "I am delighted to see you looking so well, Miss—"

He was never to complete his sentence. As the gaze of the young woman rested on Holmes' face, her whole demeanor altered in an instant. Her face paled with a suddenness that made me think she was going to faint. Instead, a scream burst from her lips, a cry that rang with hopelessness as much as terror, and echoes in my memory to this day.

Sally Craddock burst away from us and out of the little room, so swiftly and unexpectedly that neither Holmes nor I could stop her. Through the main room of the police station and the outer foyer we raced after her, as startled faces turned our way, a hue and cry went up, and other men joined in the pursuit.

Holmes was not more than two strides behind the fleet girl as she darted into the busy street, and I was running right on his heels. We both cried out a warning at the sight of the heavy dray-wagon that came rumbling toward us at high speed, but our shouts were in vain. The slender figure sped right into the path of the four powerful horses, and was run down.

The wagon hurtled on, only to overturn with a great crash as its driver tried to round the next corner without slackening speed; but neither Holmes nor I as much as turned our heads in that direction at the moment.

Bending over the crumpled body of the girl, I saw in an instant that her injuries were likely to prove fatal, and turned to call for the police to bring a stretcher. When I turned back, Holmes had knelt beside me and was silently pointing to the girl's throat. Two tiny puncture-marks stood out there, stark against the white of the girl's skin.

XV

After escorting Sally to within sight of the police station, I remained watchfully nearby until she had vanished within its protective doors. At that point I considered I had done all that honor could reasonably require of me for her present welfare, and considered myself free to turn all my thoughts and energies toward avenging us both and assuring as best I could her future safety.

According to Sally's information the building in which I had been held a prisoner was not far away, and I rose on batwings to seek it out before the dawn. I found the structure just as she had described it, an old, faceless, nameless edifice of brick a few yards from the river. I flew around it once, discovering a disappointing aura of desertion. All the doors were tight shut in those voiceless walls, the windows closely shuttered or boarded over.

Landing upon a windowsill, I melted into mist, in which form I could have passed through a crack much thinner than those offered by the warped boards before me. If the place had ever been a proper dwelling it was so no longer, and the lack of an invitation did not prevent my passage through one dark, empty room after another. I could hear the scurrying of a few ordinary rats; nothing else now breathed within those walls. The enemy, for whatever reason, had moved on. I had not the slightest doubt that I had come to the right place, for they had left behind them a considerable litter of scientific and medical equipment, including at least one of the strange carts unpleasantly familiar to me from my days of captivity.

Others in my place might have found among this debris a wealth of clues, but Matthews had been grossly wrong when he called me a detective. To me, as I stood amid that exotic litter, only one fact was plain: Dr. David Fitzroy was no longer here, and there was no reason to think he might return.

Where next to search for him and for his as yet unidentified co-conspirators? Leaning against the building's outer wall and pondering this question, I let myself be overtaken by the dawn. Unable to change shape during the hours of daylight, I thus gave up for a day the privilege of seeking out my snug earth in Mile End. But I considered that I had urgent work to do, and a tough old *nosferatu* such as I could readily endure a day or two of tempered, slanting British sunshine.

Leaving the waterfront, I sought out a used-clothing stall in Whitechapel and bought a presentable hat to replace the cap that I had somewhere lost, thus acquiring both a sunshade and some little foothold on respectability. I then spent the remainder of the morning gradually upgrading my entire wardrobe, here purchasing untattered trousers, there a better second-hand coat, in a third place some shoes without holes. By noon I was still far from the epitome of fashion, but at least felt confident of being able to enter a newspaper office or a library without being summarily thrown out.

The first library I tried offered a medical reference

book, listing a Dr. David Fitzroy . . . indeed, listing more than one. But, even if I knew which one I wanted, what good would his address be to me? This melancholy realization dawned on me as I stood tapping a taloned forefinger on the page. After what had happened at Barley's, the police must certainly be looking for my foe, and he would not be sitting at home to wait for them, nor for me either. He must be in hiding. But how was I to find out where?

Alas, sane and methodical procedures for doing anything are not really my forte. By midafternoon, the only really constructive idea that had come to me was to buy and read the newspapers, in hopes of catching some word, direct or indirect, of my enemies and their machinations. That day's papers did not reward me, nor did those of the next day, but I persisted.

Thus it came to pass that, about a week after the affair at Barley's, a lanky, slightly seedy but still respectable Continental gentleman might have been observed, hat shading his eyes against the warm late afternoon sun, seated on a park bench and somewhat pensively perusing the latest edition of the *Times*. The items successively attracting his interest ran approximately as follows:

PRECAUTION—Avoid impure water from wells and cisterns, the fertile sources of zymotic diseases. The safest and best drinking water for table, bedroom, and tea-making is the "ALPHA BRAND" . . .

ALGERNON GISSING'S NEW NOVEL
THE SCHOLAR OF BYGATE

(Algernon who? you ask. Well, such is literary fame.)

CAN any LADY RECOMMEND for the end of
September, London and country, a really first-
class PLAIN COOK? Abstainer, active, and early
riser. Age 29 to 35 (not over). Four in family,
eight servants. Quiet, very neat appearance. Also
at same time a good, strong, clean kitchenmaid,
good at vegetables. Age 18-20.

(I could sympathize, having long yearned for a staff of
really first-class servants in Castle Dracula. But one
cannot have everything.)

SPORTING INTELLIGENCE . . . (I looked under
this heading, but found nothing on rat-killing.)

. . . a minister from Stuttgart, Herr Traub, spoke
in the name of the Evangelical workmen's syndi-
cates of Wurtemburg and supported the legal eight
hours' day. He denied the assertion that workmen
would spend the extra spare time in beer drinking.

. . . the foreman of a contractor for the Post
Office was fined 5 pounds for working horses in
an unfit state . .

(From an address by Dr. William Osler) . . .
when one considers the remarkable opportunities
for study which India has presented . . . such a
field for observation in cholera, leprosy, dysen-
tery, the plague, typhoid fever, malaria . . . the
work of Dr. Hankin and of Professor Haffkine,

177

and the not unmixed evil of the brisk epidemic of plague in Bombay, may rouse the officials to a consciousness of their shortcomings . . .

(I had not seen a "brisk" epidemic of plague for more than two centuries, and had no wish to see another, though I myself am almost certainly immune.)

TELEGRAPHING WITHOUT WIRES—A large quantity of instruments, weighing in all about two tons, have arrived at Dover in connexion with some experiments in telegraphing without wires which are to be made there.

EGYPTIAN-HALL
England's home of mystery
Startling mysteries by Mr. David Devant

(I thought to myself that if I had time for amusement, I should prefer something more soothing.)

ANGLING—This week the general angling season will open . . .

TURKEY AND GREECE—The Armistice

The question of the establishment of a pneumatic post in London has been more than once under consideration . . .

THE FAMINE IN INDIA
Starving subjects of Her Majesty's Indian Empire . . .

THE DIAMOND JUBILEE. The state carriage in which the Queen will drive out June 22 will be the same as was used at the Jubilee in 1887 . . .

THE PLATTNER STORY, by H.G. Wells. A book just published . . .

(And my attention jumped back to the preceding item. June 22? That was the date mentioned by Fitzroy in my hearing as some kind of deadline. A coincidence? I pondered, but got nowhere.)

PLAN showing the berths of the MEN-OF-WAR and the track for yachts at the Jubilee naval review on June 26 . . .

MAP showing the route of the royal procession on June 22 . . .

(*The twenty-second of June draws near*, said Fitzroy's cultured voice, played back in memory. But what could the connection be?)

A GENTLEMAN is willing to LET his TWO WINDOWS for DIAMOND JUBILEE. Accommodation for about 14; use of third room for lunch. Every convenience. Double view of procession, as it passes windows and circles over London bridge. Apply C. Meredith, 78 King William street, City.

(A column was filled with similar advertisements.)

THE KLONDIKE GOLD REEFS
EXPLORATION COMPANY, LIMITED
APPLICATION FOR SHARES . . .

COCKLE'S PILLS . . .

THE ADVANCE ON THE NILE . . .

NESTLE'S MILK . . .

National Society for Prevention of Cruelty to
Children . . .

CHEAP RETURN TICKETS TO THE EAST
—India, Ceylon, China, Australia, Tasmania—

AT WORSHIP-STREET, POLICE-CON-
STABLE FRANKLIN, 4436, appeared to
answer a summons charging him with violently
assaulting Mary Smith and causing her actual bodily harm. The complainant, a tall, powerfully-
built Irishwoman, said that . . . she was in Mans-
field-street, Kingsland-road, going home, and
met the policeman, who "shoved" against her,
asked her what luck she had had that night, and
made overtures to her. When she rejected them
. . . he kicked her . . . hit her in the left eye and
burst the ball . . .

HUMPHREYS' PORTABLE IRON
CHURCHES, Chapels, Mission, Club, Reading
and School Rooms, Cottages . . .

BABY HAGAR, 29, a respectably-dressed young

woman, said to be an actress, was charged with attempted suicide. Evidence was given by Inspector Chandler of the Thames Police, that on Saturday evening he saw accused struggling in the Thames near Waterloo-bridge. On getting her out of the water she told him, "I have had but one glass of port wine, and I jumped from the bridge because I was tired of life." Mr. Hall, the Court missionary, informed the magistrate that prisoner told him she had been unfortunate in her employment and had got very low down and despondent. On his advice she promised to apply to the Ladies' Theatrical Guild . . .

St. Marylebone FEMALE PROTECTION SOCIETY, 157-9, Marylebone-road, NW. This Society seeks to rescue young women who up to the time of their fall have borne a good character. Those with infants are assisted from a special fund. CONTRIBUTIONS are earnestly solicited.

(I could envision a dedicated corps, perhaps neatly uniformed, standing guard with boats and ropes and life-preservers, below all the bridges of the Thames. But neither I nor Baby Hagar had seen them there, and I understood that my vision must fall short of the truth somehow.)

ELLIMAN'S UNIVERSAL EMBROCATION "THE ONLY GENUINE RUB ON THE MARKET"

National Society for Checking the Abuses of Public Advertising . . .

DU BARRY'S REVALENTA ARABICA FOOD "It has cured me of 9 years' constipation, declared beyond cure by the best physicians, and given me new life, health, and happiness.—A. Spadaro, Merchant, Alexandria, Egypt."

THE SEXAGENARY OF PHONOG-RAPHY . . .

(This proved to be not as interesting an article as my first glance at the headline led me to hope.)

THE COAL MINERS' STRIKE IN AMERICA . . .

PEARS' SOAP . . .

WAGES IN THE COTTON INDUSTRY—The replies from cotton manufacturers in Blackburn, Burnley, and Preston as to a proposed reduction in weavers' wages of 10 per cent., &c., were return-able yesterday, but the committee will not consider them finally or seriously until next Friday . . .

HUNYADI JANOS the BEST and SAFEST NATURAL APERIENT . . . free from de-fects incidental to many other Hungarian Bitter Waters . . .

(That friend and ally of my breathing days, Janos Hunyadi, *voivode* of Transylvania and later ruler of all Hungary, would have found these waters bitter to his taste indeed.)

COMPETITION for WORD to ADVERTISE a GINGER ALE—"G.S.C." begs to notify competitors that it has not been possible to settle this matter yet, and requests any who may have an opportunity of disposing of their word in another direction to do so. The result will be advertised as soon as a decision is come to.

CHESS
THE INTERNATIONAL CONGRESSS IN BERLIN
The 4th round in the chess tournament was begun this morning. M. Tschigorin played against Mr. Blackburne, but, losing his queen through oversight, gave up after 25 moves . . .

MERRYWEATHER'S latest Domestic Novelty is their PATENT PORTABLE ELECTRIC FIRE ENGINE for Corridors of Mansions and Institutions having Electric Light, by the utilization of the Electric Current to actuate the fire pump.

SALVATION ARMY . . . there are baths, hot and cold, at all our shelters, and they are largely used . . . all are not admitted who apply . . .
                    W. BRAMWELL BOOTH

(I blessed my good fortune that I had somehow qualified in my hour of need, and reminded myself to send a large, anonymous donation when I again possessed the means.)

BICYCLE POLO at CRYSTAL PALACE
This new game is played without mallets . . .

Steamers from Panama are now given clean bills
of health, and are no longer subject to quarantine
in Equatorian and Peruvian ports . . .

NATIONAL TRUSS SOCIETY for the RELIEF
of the RUPTURED POOR . . .

. . . at WORSHIP-STREET, a sturdy little boy,
very ragged and barefooted, was charged by a
school attendance officer with wandering and with
not being under proper guardianship . . . there
seems to be a large floating population increasing
constantly . . .

. . . the Dreyfus affair is assuming larger propor-
tions . . .

IT IS A FACT!
THAT MUCH MEAT EATING produces mus-
cular rheumatism, gout, severe pains in the limbs
and joints, cold extremities, clamminess, weak
circulation, Migraine (headache)
AND oftentimes *corpulence*. People say 'the
blood is the life', but such a statement is nonsense . . .

(Indeed?)

THE PLAGUE IN INDIA—A *minimum* quarantine of six days is being enforced against all 2nd
and 3rd class arrivals by rail at Bombay from

plague-infected areas . . . four more Europeans attacked by plague were admitted to hospital at Poona yesterday . . .

THE GREAT HORSELESS CARRIAGE CO., LTD. . . .

(I had heard fragments of information concerning such machines, but had yet to see one.)

BARNUM & BAILEY—Greatest show on Earth—Opening in Great Olympia . . .

THE DIAMOND JUBILEE LACE SHIRT . . .

FOUND—A very large traveler's trunk, locked, of fine heavy leather, and Continental manufacture. The owner may have same by identifying the name attached . . .

I read that last item through twice, then stood up, folding my paper. It seemed that perhaps the bitch-goddess was going to smile on me again; and high time, too, I thought.

That night as soon as dusk had fallen I was at the given address in Westminster, having meanwhile spent some of my last coins purchasing a better hat, one which even Monsieur Corday of Paris and Vienna need not feel ashamed of wearing.

The sturdy, middle-aged woman who answered the door was polite enough, but very firm in her refusal to let me enter. She remained unimpressed by what I considered my most ingratiating smile. I would have to return in the morning, she said, when the party who had found the trunk—no, she did not know where or how it had been found—would probably be in.

Two hours after a gloomy sunrise, I was back. The same stolid woman ushered me upstairs to a somewhat exotic sitting-room, in one corner of which sat a great trunk, unmistakably mine—it was fashioned of thick brown leather, and massive as a coffin, though not so distinctively shaped.

A glance told me that the name-tag had been removed, but the lid was still tightly closed, and the great box appeared to be undamaged. Scarcely had the landlady departed, leaving me in a chair to await my benefactor, when I was on my feet again and bending over my property. I had just ascertained that the trunk was still locked, when I heard soft stirrings of human life somewhere behind me, as of several people entering an adjacent room. These sounds I ignored, until a door at my back began to open quietly.

I turned, smiling to greet my benefactor, only to behold three men, two of them holding pistols aimed in my direction whilst the third gripped some kind of cudgel. In a moment, an exceptionally lovely young woman had come through the door behind them, and stood there gazing at me as at an enemy.

The thin, intense man who was poised a little in advance of all the others said: "These weapons, sir, are for our own protection only."

"Indeed?" I responded. "Even with odds of three to one? What makes you think I mean you harm—and why are you all so timid on this fine June morning?" The clouds of dawn had blown away, and somewhere in a garden birds were twittering.

"We were more timid, still, in last night's darkness," he answered, and in his voice there was a meaning that I with great foolishness left unread. With casual contempt I turned my back on them, and bent once more to the examination of my trunk.

And I froze in that position, when he added in an incisive tone: "Let us play games no longer. I shall be greatly pleased to hear from your own lips, Count Dracula, the truth of how Frau Grafenstein came to her end."

XVI

We carried Sally Craddock straight to hospital from where she had been struck down. For several hours she lingered, Holmes and I both remaining at her bedside, and then she died without regaining consciousness. Meanwhile the driver of the dray-wagon was apprehended, but as he had been himself very severely injured in the capsizing of his vehicle, he was in no condition to be seriously questioned. Holmes recognized him at once as a minor criminal and bully.

"Of course they knew she was in the station, Watson—somehow they knew. This choice specimen was assigned to wait outside, and was quick enough to seize his chance when it came. I feel responsible for giving him that chance. I did not foresee that Sally Craddock would see the vampire's face in mine, or would react as she did to the sight."

"How could you have foreseen anything of the kind? In her brief statement to the police she described the— the killer—as being friendly and helpful to her. 'Gentlemanly' was another word she used, was it not?" Lestrade had brought a copy of her first and only declaration to the hospital for us to see.

Holmes shook his head. "I should have suspected,

though, that he might have inspired in her a fear and loathing that ran very deep.* It is the other side of the coin of the damnable attractiveness that these creatures possess for women. Those punctures on her throat were not made by horses' hooves or a wagon's wheels.''

To this I suppose I must have stammered some reply. Shortly thereafter I returned to Baker Street, while Holmes hurled himself with feverish energy into activities of which I was able to observe only a small part. He was in and out of our lodgings repeatedly for the rest of the day. On each return he asked if there were any messages, and replied to my own questions brusquely if at all.

It was evening before he came in and stayed long enough to make it worthwhile taking off his hat. He threw himself into a chair, sought solace in strong tobacco, and altogether gave an impression of deep, struggling thought combined with near-exhaustion. I prevailed upon him to take a little food, and shortly thereafter, to my great relief, he retired, very early, for the night.

That night I found myself unable to sleep much. Up early the following morning, I peeped in cautiously on Holmes and saw with satisfaction that he still slumbered.

I had just finished my breakfast when two gentlemen were announced, and it was with some surprise that I greeted Lord Godalming and Dr. Seward. I had not seen them and had scarcely thought of them since the

*The whole question of Sally Craddock's true motive in fleeing the police station, if it is to be raised at all, deserves more space than is here available. I will only remark that it is a large assumption to make, that Watson *invariably* records Holmes' statements accurately.—D.

affair at Barley's. Looking now at their faces, which were both somewhat grimly set, I asked: "May I take it, gentlemen, that this visit is not purely social?"

"It is not." Jack Seward exchanged glances with his companion, then went on: "Our business concerns a matter of great delicacy, but I am sure you will understand that it is one which cannot be allowed to pass in silence."

"Perhaps it is Sherlock Holmes whom you really wish to see. I am afraid he is not available for consultation at present." When I ordered breakfast, I had taken it upon myself to instruct Mrs. Hudson to tell any unfamiliar callers that Holmes was out.

"No, it is you we wish to see, Dr. Watson," Lord Godalming put in. "The fact is, we made sure that you were alone before we came up."

With my nerves already under strain, I found their stiff, mysterious manner quite unpleasant. "Well, then?"

Again they looked at each other hesitantly. Then Seward bluntly came out with it. "We should like to know why you interfered, that night at Barley's, with a policeman in the performance of his duty."

For a moment, my irritation threatened to burst up into anger; but quickly I saw that such an attitude was scarcely fair. In Seward's place I might well have chosen to take exactly the same course with an old acquaintance. I nodded silently.

Seward said unhappily: "It's more, of course, than just a matter of the man escaping an arrest for gambling, or anything of that kind. I believe, Watson, that this fellow was actually the Thames-side murderer."

"What has caused you to believe that?"

"Well, one has friends, you know. And some of

mine have friends at Scotland Yard. Do you deny that you helped him to get out?"

"No, I do not. But I do offer you my solemn word, gentlemen, that my intentions were of the best. If you will not accept my unsupported word, I suggest that you ask Mr. Sherlock Holmes about the matter when he awakens."

Seward blinked at me. "But the landlady said—"

"She had her orders from me. Last night I felt it my duty as Mr. Holmes' physician to administer a sedative."

My old acquaintance shook his head, expressing what was evidently a mixture of shock, embarrassment, and relief. He removed his eyeglasses and polished them and put them back. "Look here, Watson—if you say it's all square, what you were doing there at Barley's—what we thought we saw you doing, I mean—oh, dash it all, that's good enough for me. I've no real head for these detective investigations and intrigues anyway. What do you say, Arthur?"

His Lordship, also looking relieved, muttered something in the way of an agreement. When my visitors had taken the chairs I now made haste to offer them, and had courteously declined my offers of refreshment, Seward went on to inquire: "Now—I trust you will not think it unethical of me to ask—but I hope there is nothing seriously wrong with Mr. Holmes? If there is, it will give cause for rejoicing to the criminal element in this country—in all of Europe—but it will be a sad day for the rest of us."

"I . . ." I rubbed my forehead, not knowing what course I ought to take. "I have given some thought to consulting a specialist on his behalf."

Lord Godalming stood up. "It was most pleasant to

see you again, Dr. Watson. Jack, I think I shall just be on my way, and leave the matters medical, if there are to be any, to you two."

I bade His Lordship good-bye. Then, as soon as we were alone, Seward said to me gravely: "I of course stand ready to listen at any time, on a professional and confidential basis, should you desire to consult with me."

With some reluctance I began to set forth, in a stumbling fashion, my growing concern for my friend's sanity. Besides my reluctance, there was the real difficulty of my not daring to reveal, even under the cloak of professional secrecy, the terrible threat of plague hanging over London.

I began: "There is a case Holmes has presently under investigation—I had better say several connected cases—of an importance transcending anything that has come before them in his career."

"Ah." Seward was naturally impressed. "And you feel the extraordinary strain is telling on him?"

"Yes."

"How close to a solution would you say he is, in this intricate problem? Or is it more than one problem that affects him? I fear I did not take your meaning on that point very clearly."

"And I am afraid that I cannot be plainer, even in a medical consultation."

He gave me a sharp look, then shrugged. "Well, if you cannot. What symptoms precisely does he exhibit?"

Some time passed before I struggled out with it, or tried to. "There is one of the men involved . . . a fugitive . . . Holmes has become dreadfully obsessed with this individual's identity."

"Surely it is a detective's business to ascertain that?"

"I see I am expressing myself badly. Holmes has solemnly assured me, more than once, that this man—it is the very one I unwittingly helped at Barley's—is a—a type of supernatural being."

"The man at Barley's—I see." Seward leaned back in his chair, looking grave. "By the way, I have heard that the girl arrested there has lately been severely injured. Do not think, Watson, that I am going too far afield in asking these questions. They have a bearing on the nature of Mr. Holmes' difficulty."

"No doubt they do." Holmes had asked that Sally Craddock's death be kept a secret, so far as possible. "But had I not better first describe the patient's condition?"

"Of course, if you wish. Precisely what type of supernatural being does Mr. Holmes imagine this fugitive to be?"

I had to come out with it at last. "A vampire."

Seward looked so grave* at this that my spirits, which had begun to rise at the prospect of acquiring an ally, were crushed again. He asked: "What turn have his investigations taken, to put such an idea into his head?"

"I repeat, I cannot discuss them—I could not, even

*Those readers who have seen my own recent account of my London visit in 1891, or my enemies' old distorted record of the same events, will have already recognized Dr. Seward and Lord Godalming, as two of my opponents on that occasion. The existence of vampires would therefore have been no news to either man in 1897—though, being jealous of their own reputations for sanity, they were not likely to discuss their knowledge with outsiders. And whether Seward first conceived the possibility that I was still alive and back in London during this talk with Watson, or at some other moment, it must have struck him like a red-hot lash.—D.

to save his sanity. You consider, then, that delusions regarding vampires are particularly morbid?''

"I consider that it may be very difficult to save his sanity, unless I know what threatens it. At the same time I must of course respect your decision regarding the relative importance of matters of which I know nothing.''

"I wish I could tell you more, but I cannot. Holmes should awaken soon, if you would care to—''

"No, Watson, I think not. I should prefer that he not discover just yet that you have been holding medical consultation on his behalf without his knowledge. What sedative have you prescribed?'' At my reply he nodded thoughtfully. "It seems to be strong enough to help him rest; and perhaps rest will suffice.''

"You really think so?''

"Let us give it a chance. If you think some stronger sedative is indicated, here is a sample of a South American drug I have found invaluable in cases of nervous exhaustion. It induces mental relaxation and a deep sleep without deleterious side-effects.'' After groping in his pockets for a moment, Seward produced a small, plain box, which he opened to show me a single pill. "One dose is all I have with me at the moment; but the patient should have no more than one in a twenty-four hour period, and if you desire more you have but to call on me.''

I accepted the box with thanks, and put it in my own pocket. Seward tore a page from his pocket-book and began scribbling on it. "Here is the address of my establishment in Purfleet—this is the telephone number, should you have the opportunity of getting to an instrument to call. Please do so at once, should there be any outbreak of violent or frantic behavior by the patient, or if for any other reason you wish my assistance. All the facilities of my asylum are of course at your disposal if the need arises, which we must hope it does not. Members of some of the most eminent families in Britain have been among my patients there. I have been thinking lately of giving up the old place and re-settling elsewhere, so there are few or no patients in residence at the moment—all to the good in this case, where we'd certainly want privacy. Some old friends are in from Exeter for the Jubilee, but they have visited before and know the rules, and so should present no problem."

Seward soon departed, bearing with him my heartfelt thanks. Left alone again, I felt distinctly better for having unburdened my mind, and, as I hoped, gained an able partner in my struggle on Holmes' behalf.

He was up not long after, and looked better for his long rest, though he rubbed his eyes on entering the sitting-room, and actually stumbled momentarily against me. This dazed condition quickly passed, however, and his manner was alert as he looked about him. "I see we have had visitors," was his first comment.

"Two acquaintances of mine," I answered, relieved that my friend gave no sign of being aware that I had administered a drug to him by means of last night's curried chicken.

Evidently Holmes' thoughts had already passed on to other matters. "I must return this morning, Watson, to an old acquaintance of mine whom I visited briefly yesterday—no doubt you remember the blind German mechanic, Von Herder?"

"Of course—the man who built air-guns for Colonel Sebastian Moran, of evil memory. Do you go to visit the blind man in prison?"

"No." Holmes smiled to see my quick expression of concern. "Nor is the blind man still to be counted among my enemies. Since he has quite reformed, he has come to live in London; a change of address which I had some small hand in arranging for him, and for which he has been kind enough to express his gratitude, by placing his skills at my disposal. In fact, I expect that he has been at work for me all night."

"If you go to see him, I shall come with you."

"That is impossible. His reformation is quite genuine, but the presence of someone he does not know is likely to upset him." Holmes fell abruptly silent. He was standing at the window, so that for a moment I thought he had spied something of unusual interest in the street. But then he said, without turning: "Do you remember, Watson? It was the sight of my face that sent her running, screaming, to her death."

"Of course I remember, Holmes. But it was not your fault."

He turned to face me. "Have you thought about vampires, Watson, as I urged you?"

"Yes." It was an unwilling answer, and I was agreeably distracted by the arrival of the girl with the breakfast which Holmes had ordered on awakening.

"Good, very good!" He sounded almost hearty. "When the time comes, I must have with me someone I can trust." And he sat down and attacked his bacon and eggs with an energy that gave me hope.

When the girl was safely out of hearing again, I said: "You may of course trust me in this."

His eyes fastened on mine with a suddenly alert suspicion. "Watson, you must pledge me this instant, upon your honor, that you will never mention the subject of vampires to my brother Mycroft; it is the one thing that would undo him utterly. Have I your pledge?''

"You have," I answered in a heavy voice, and with the gravest mental reservations. Actually I had been considering for some time that circumstances might very soon oblige me to consult with Mycroft. As most of my readers may know, Holmes' older brother was, to the best of my knowledge, his next of kin—indeed, his only living relative. Mycroft was employed by the Government, and never left London. So constant were his habits, in fact, that I had put off consulting him, feeling that I should have no trouble locating him for that purpose at any hour of the day or night.

Some train of thought begun with Mycroft had plunged Holmes into an introspective pause, almost a reverie, his plate of food abandoned before him as if he had suddenly forgotten it.

"I have never spoken to you of my childhood, have I, Watson?"

"No, Holmes, you never have."

"There were painful things in it, which I suppose is common enough. But not such things . . . at any rate, Mycroft's childhood must have been worse, for he was seven years my senior, and must have seen more, and understood more at the time. I am referring to things one might think too horrible for any child to bear. Therefore the effects upon him were more severe than upon myself. I must warn you again, the mere mention of vampires could destroy him.''

I waited, listening attentively, which is often the best thing a doctor can do for any patient.

Holmes went on, in the same distracted tone: "My father was, as I think I have mentioned, a country squire. A kindly man, of considerable intelligence,

THE HOLMES-DRACULA FILE

though little fame. Also he was a man of great strength, for he survived . . . much.''

I waited still.

When Holmes resumed again, his voice had taken on the strain that of late had become all too frequent in it. "You know that Mycroft and I have both devoted our lives to intellectual pursuits. And neither of us has married . . .''

I had the strong impression that my friend was trembling upon the brink of some revelation or confession, which in prospect seemed to me likely to be terrible—the more terrible inasmuch as I could not for the life of me imagine what it might be, or whether, indeed, it would have any basis at all but the fancies engendered in a disordered brain.

At this crucial moment we were interrupted by the bell. When I came back with telegram in hand, I saw with mixed feelings of relief and disappointment that in the brief interval my friend had pulled himself together, and the revelation was not to come.

The telegram was from Superintendent Marlowe, addressed to Holmes, who promptly tore it open, and read it with an expression of satisfaction.

"He has, as you may recall, Watson, a whole chain of warehouses under his direction; and this communication is in reply to one of my own, asking Mr. Marlowe in which building I should be likely to find a very large box or trunk, unloaded on or about the tenth of this month from some ship arriving at the East India docks from Mediterranean ports, and unclaimed by the owner. I shall be surprised now if we cannot put our hands on this piece of baggage in a matter of hours, and with luck we shall see its owner in a day or two.''

"A trunk? I do not see—"

"Are you ready to go out, Watson? Action is required. The game is afoot, and moves more quickly than I had anticipated."

XVII

As soon as I had recovered from the shock of being thus addressed by my true name, I turned to study more carefully the four people who confronted me. Only as I did so did I recognize, at the right hand of their leader and half a step behind him, the strongly-built man who had so mysteriously and opportunely come to my aid at Barley's. He had impressed me then as brave; now his brow was furrowed, though not, I thought, with any fear of me. He kept darting glances at the dominant figure of his chief, and bit his mustache as if in worry.

The third man was quite young, and almost tremulous—I dismissed him, and my gaze moved on, to rest on the young woman. It would perhaps be an exaggeration to write that all idea of danger was at once swept from my mind. Let me say instead that her presence placed before me so strongly all of life's joyous possibilities, that its cares and even its perils appeared much diminished in importance.

"Your look mocks me, sir," she said, with hardly any tremor in her voice, while her eyes boldly met mine.

My admiration was increased. "Nay, I never mock beauty, and still less courage," I replied. And now at last I locked my gaze against their leader's. He reminded me of someone—I could not at first think who. "Fair warning," I added. "Do not fire those guns at me."

"As I have said," he answered, "they are for our own protection only. And now, Count, the truth, if you please, about Frau Grafenstein."

"Are you a policeman? Even so, I will not countenance your meddling in my affairs."

"I know that you killed that woman, and that you drank her blood." It was a prosecutor's voice.

"I was extremely thirsty," I responded, and saw the youngest and least steady of the men turn half away, shaking his head and muttering something to himself about the mother of his God.

My violent demise, when it comes, will doubtless be attributable to my own overweening pride. With fine contempt I turned my back upon them all, and reached out again toward my trunk, thinking to pick it up and carry it away at once. The sound of the pistol behind me was quite loud within the four confining walls. Across my left forearm, extended to grip a handle of my box, a white-hot iron was laid, or rather smashed with numbing force. For a moment I believed that my arm had been utterly mangled, and I am afraid that I stared like a dunce at the sudden drip and flow of my own red blood along my wrist and fingers.

But the arm, though punctured, was still essentially intact. Once more I turned, and looked into the unflinching eyes behind the smoking pistol-barrel. "My congratulations," I offered, "on thinking of wooden bullets. I had begun to believe all Englishmen were fools." Now that my eyes were opened, I could see that what I had taken for a crude club in the hands of the youngest man was in fact a finely-pointed wooden stake.

My chief opponent—indeed, the only one of the four worthy of the name—bowed slightly, without relaxing either his aim or his alertness for an instant. "My apologies, Count," he murmured, "but I considered it necessary to demonstrate at once the effectiveness of our weapons and the firmness of our purpose, lest you should force us to put them immediately to the ultimate test. I should be disappointed if I have no chance to talk with you before anything of that sort occurs. Do you require medical aid?"

I only smiled. The girl sharply drew in her breath. The young man shrank back half a step, then, as if ashamed of this reaction, moved forward until he stood an inch or two closer to me than before.

But still it was only to the leader that I spoke. "Of course I will talk with you. For this *contretemps* in which I find myself I have only myself to blame, Mr.—?"

"Allow me to remedy the lack of formal introductions all round. Count Dracula, Dr. Watson, Mr. Peter Moore of New York—Miss Sarah Tarlton, also an American. And my name is Sherlock Holmes."

Holmes' name was of course at that time widely known, in Europe and indeed across the world, and he spoke it with the air of a man quietly and confidently playing a trump card. Alas for the isolation of my Translyvanian backwater, which I had so rarely left! The utter blankness with which I received the name of Holmes must have struck his proud nature with something of the force of deliberate insult.

At the moment I only knew, without realizing why, that he had suddenly gone a little pale. "Watson," he grated, "Moore—Miss Tarlton. You will please leave me alone with this man, at once."

Watson was considerably agitated. "Holmes," he whispered, "Holmes, let me fetch Lestrade."

"Very well," Holmes agreed, somewhat (as I thought) to Watson's surprise. "Only leave us, immediately!"

Young Moore stumbled as he backed toward the exit, his horrified and fascinated eyes never leaving my face. Sarah Tarlton turned her back on me and walked out with alacrity, as if guided by some instinct to seek the more wholesome world beyond the door. Watson made a methodical retreat. His last perturbed glance as he went out was toward his leader.

Perhaps they were all too well accustomed to taking Holmes' orders to question this one, or even try to understand its purpose. But I—I understood. When the next shot was fired, there were to be no witnesses.

XVIII

As my friend and I drove east through the city again, in response to the telegram from Superintendent Marlowe, I asked: "Even if we are right to assume that the man did recently arrive in London by ship, how are we to distinguish his baggage from that of a thousand others?"

Holmes smiled. "I have not told you yet of my interview with the informer, Jones. The peculiar man Jones met in the hostel actually asked him where unclaimed luggage from the East India docks would be taken. Jones could not provide the information, but fortunately we have the means of finding it out."

"Jones told Lestrade of this also?"

"He did."

"But the police have made no effort to follow up this clue?"

"Lestrade only shakes his head, and shares your doubts about the possibility of distinguishing the baggage that is wanted. But—if my hopes are justified—it will be distinguishable because it is unique. What does a vampire need, Watson? What does he need even more than the blood he drains to slake his fearful appetite?"

With my heart sinking, as it did each time evidence of Holmes' unfortunate mental state was forced upon me, I muttered and mumbled something to the effect that I did not know.

"His earth, Watson! Some nest of the snug soil of his homeland, for in nothing else can he find rest. If we do not find a large trunk or box containing earth, then my hopes are not justified, and our quarry is a vampire native of England, merely returning from abroad with commonplace luggage of dirty laundry and spare shoes. Oh, they are human, you know, in many ways. Damnably like us, except . . ." Holmes' voice trailed off. His hands were both tightly clenched on the grip of a large carpetbag he had brought along from Baker Street, and he looked as grim as I had ever seen him. "But, if we do find a trunk filled with earth, in that moment a great cloud will lift from my mind."

"Then your wish to find it," I put in impulsively, "cannot be stronger than my own."

"Good old Watson! You are speaking sincerely in that much, at least. No, never mind about the rest. In time you will be convinced—I pray that the time is not too late."

Soon we were rolling to a stop at our destination, a Thames-side warehouse much like the one in which we had first met Superintendent Marlowe, and not far distant from it. Inside the building, we found him with two workmen, amid a huge pile of baggage of every description.

Marlowe, electric lamp in hand, was standing before a huge, brown leather trunk. "We have followed your instructions to the letter, Mr. Holmes," he announced by way of greeting. "This is the only thing of its size brought in as unclaimed this past month from the East India docks. It is locked, you see, and we have done nothing in the way of trying to open it."

"Excellent!" Holmes turned over the tag appended to the chest, which had only a light film of dust upon its surface. The tag was marked with the name M. Corday, and showed that the trunk had been shipped within the month from Marseilles to London.

"It's large enough to hold a body, as you said," the superintendent offered, while the eyes of the workmen widened as they listened. "You think, sir, that's what's in it?"

"Our task will be much simpler if it is. Kindly move it over here to the center of the open floor."

As if nerving himself for an ordeal, Holmes now drew from his pocket a small metal pick, and with this he attacked the lock. I saw a fine tremor in his hands, and twice his tool slipped from the narrow keyhole. His face was a mask of great restraint. At last, seeming to master his nerves by a supreme effort of will, he succeeded in working the mechanism.

The faint click of the lock was followed by a long moment in which he did not move at all. Then he stood up and with a violent motion flung back the lid. What precisely he had expected or feared to see within, I did not know, but I saw his shoulders slump with the sudden release of tension. And as I peered over his shoulder I saw to my own amazement that the great leather chest was half-filled with what appeared to be nothing but blackish dirt.

"It is as I hoped, Watson," Holmes breathed, and the great relief in his voice was as evident as it was mysterious to me. "Our killer is not a native of England, for he has brought his nest with him."

Opening the large carpetbag he had brought with him in the cab, my friend, to my astonishment, pulled from it a large stake of some hard wood, two feet long and about two inches thick, with one end sharpened to an almost needle-like point, and charred as if it had been hardened in a fire. With the point of this stake he began to probe down into the earth within the trunk, on the first few attempts hitting nothing resistant before reaching the bottom. On the next try, however, he gave a little grunt of satisfaction, laid aside the stake, rolled up one sleeve, and plunged his sinewy arm into the soil.

He pulled out a snug bundle that, when brushed off and unrolled on the warehouse floor, proved to be a large waterproof, in which had been wrapped two or three complete suits of men's clothing, a collapsible top-hat, soap and towels, a pair of boots, a clothes-brush, and a heavy purse. From this last, when Holmes had opened it, there poured out a substantial amount of bank-notes and coin, the latter predominantly gold.

Each of these items Holmes picked up and studied, briefly but with a feverish eagerness. "There is light in the darkness, Watson," he cried almost joyously. "The danger is far from past, but so far all the signs are hopeful."

Leaving Marlowe and his men to shake their heads in wonder, I, following Holmes' terse orders, saw the trunk and its contents conveyed to Baker Street, and there lodged in a corner of our sitting room. Holmes himself meanwhile hurried away on the errand he had already mentioned, an unexplained visit to our former foe, Von Herder.

By lunch time he was back in Baker Street, where to my complete surprise his first act was to hand me half a dozen cartridges. "These should fit your old service revolver nicely, Watson." I thought that when I weighed the casings in my hand they felt surprisingly light, and the bullets where they protruded from the brass were a strange, dull brown.

Seeing my puzzlement, Holmes nodded. "Yes, Watson, they are wood. They would not do, I fear, for long shots on the pistol range, but they are just what we want to defend ourselves during the task at hand. Kindly load your revolver with them immediately." His manner was now keen and eager as of old, without a trace of that inward agony that had lately given me such concern. I might have been relieved at this change, were it not that he gave no indication of changing his conviction that it was a vampire we were hunting.

On the contrary, Holmes soon summoned Mrs. Hudson, and gave her orders in the strictest terms. "A visitor will sooner or later call, in regard to this most impressive trunk. You are to admit no one—no man, woman, or child, no one at all, regardless of what reasons they may urge—who comes upon such an errand after nightfall. Who applies at night must be told to come back in the morning."

"Very good, sir."

When the landlady had gone, Holmes showed me the advertisement describing the trunk that he had placed in all the papers, and with that we settled down to wait. A day passed, and then another, none without some secret inquiry from the highest levels of government, regarding the threat of plague. Holmes curtly put off all official questions, and spent his time largely smoking, fiddling, or staring out the window.

For my part, I scarcely knew which way to turn. Had it not been for my friend's success in finding the trunkful of earth exactly as he had predicted it would be found, I should probably have decided to confide in

Mycroft, and, with his approval, confront the highest authorities with our opinion that Holmes was no longer competent, by reason of an unbalanced mind.

Yet—there sat the trunk, inexplicably half-filled with soil. Had not Sherlock Holmes, even partially unbalanced, intellectual powers far beyond those of any other detective, powers that must be utilized if England were to be saved?

"He must come, Watson, he must come," Holmes muttered to me, over and over, in intervals of impatient pacing. It was night, some days after the trunk had been first advertised. "Though it now seems certain that he must have at least one other earth somewhere in London. Or is it possible that he is dead? We have heard nothing of him for some—"

The bell downstairs rang faintly, and Holmes stopped in mid-stride, finger to his lips. I, just risen from my chair to tend the fire, stayed where I was, listening with might and main. Very faintly I could hear Mrs. Hudson's voice below, and then felt the slight change in the draught that resulted from the closing of the downstairs door. Nothing else, until her familiar tread sounded gently on the stair, and she came in to give us her report. "It was a foreign-sounding gentleman, sir, very polite, asking about the trunk. I did just as you ordered."

Holmes was at one of the window-blinds, making sure that it was drawn shut to the last fraction of an inch. He came back close to our landlady before whispering: "And who is now in the house besides ourselves?"

"Why, just the servant girl, sir."

"Admit no one else tonight—much may depend upon it."

"Very good, sir."

When she had gone, Holmes said to me: "As for you, old fellow, he might well recognize you from Barley's. I must insist that you do not go out tonight."

"Agreed, provided you do not."

"I agree. And now it is time to get some sleep—we will have to be up and about at dawn."

The gray light of sunrise found us in the sitting-room once more. Holmes was heating coffee on his spirit-lamp, and examining his own revolver, when a sudden sharp jangle at the bell set my nerves to vibrating. Following Holmes' silent, urgent motions, I went with him into his room, where we closed the door to the sitting-room and waited, guns drawn and ready, literally holding our breath.

The door to the stair opened, and there was movement in the sitting-room—but the voices coming through to us were those of Peter Moore and Sarah Tarlton. I felt suddenly limp, and I saw Holmes slump, only to bristle again in vexation. Jamming his revolver into a pocket of his dressing-gown, he opened the bedroom door.

Sarah Tarlton turned to him with a glad little cry. "Mr. Holmes, I am glad that you are in at last. For several days we have been trying to see you, and—"

"And you have been told that I was out. Well, you are here now and there is no help for it. Was anyone outside in the street just now when you came in?"

Our visitors both looked puzzled. "Anyone?" Peter Moore replied. "I scarcely noticed."

Holmes shook his head and rubbed his eyes, muttering something that none of us—perhaps fortunately—could hear. "Both of you," he added, "were, like Watson, at Barley's on that night. So now that you are here, here you must stay."

"Stay? I am afraid I do not understand."

"We are in the process of trying to trap—the bell again! Quickly, into my room."

We all four crowded into Holmes' bedroom, where he in a hurried whisper tried to impart to our visitors as much knowledge of the coming confrontation as was practicable under the circumstances. To my relief, he did not mention vampires. Still Miss Tarlton paled a little, I thought, at the sight of our drawn revolvers. Peter Moore offered his help, and Holmes plunged an arm into his carpetbag and brought out the stake, which the young American accepted with a puzzled look but a determined grip, holding it like a club.

"Do you mean," Moore asked, "that this is the man who killed John?"

"I fear not. But perhaps even more dangerous—hist!"

The outer door to our sitting-room was opened, and we heard two people enter, and the voice of Mrs. Hudson, calmly bidding a visitor to be seated. Then she went out and the door closed.

Holmes, as silent as a stalking cat, waited a few seconds and then eased open the bedroom door and stepped through it. I was right behind him, and right after me came Peter Moore. I thought I could recognize the lone occupant of the sitting-room as the tall, lean man from Barley's, though he was garbed now in better clothing, and had his back to us, stooping over the trunk as if to examine it. At the sound of our entry he straightened up and turned, and there was no longer any possible doubt. The likeness to Holmes' face was quite as strong as I remembered it, as was the suggestion of ravaged nobility.

Holmes spoke first. "These weapons, sir, are for our own protection only."

"Indeed? Even with odds of three to one on your side?" It was a deep voice, and that of an educated man who spoke English well; yet it was not an English voice. I should have put the speaker's origin somewhere in Central Europe. Looking at our guns with a smile as of superior amusement, he went on: "And why are you all so timid on this bright morning?"

"We were more timid, still, last night," Holmes answered. Before he could say more, our latest visitor, with a sneer that showed his complete contempt for all of us, had turned his back and was once more bent over the trunk as if to continue his examination of the lock.

Holmes paled at this, and his voice when he went on had a smooth, deadly tone that I have seldom heard in it, and never without grave consequences for the person spoken to. "Let us play games no longer, Count Dracula. I shall be greatly pleased to hear from your own lips the story of how Frau Grafenstein came to her end."

It was evident from the sudden complete stillness of the figure before us that this shot had told. Then he turned to face us once again, straightening deliberately to full height. The newcomer glared now at each of us in turn, as if to make sure which was most worthy of his anger. His face was almost impassive, save for the eyes, but I could see his long, sharp-nailed fingers working slightly, as if their owner imagined them already fastened on our throats. His voice when he spoke was even deeper than before. "Gentlemen, I give you fair warning—do not fire those guns at me."

"I repeat," Holmes snapped, "that they are for our

own protection only. And now, if you please, the truth about that killing on the docks.''

"I do not tolerate meddling in my affairs, even by the police. They are not your concern."

"I make them my concern, and I tell you that I already know very much about them. That you killed Frau Grafenstein, for example, and that you drank her blood."

The man before us answered clearly: "I was extremely thirsty." In a flash it was borne in upon me what I should never have forgotten. That the question of Holmes' mental state entirely aside, we had already seen ample evidence that the man we now confronted must be utterly and violently mad. There was no reason, as I abruptly realized, that one capable of that horrible killing on the docks might not *imagine himself to be a vampire*, and even carry matters to the extent of traveling about Europe with a trunk half-filled with earth.

He turned away again, with a fine demonstration of contempt, and bent as if he meant to lift the massive trunk unaided. Nothing in my long association with Sherlock Holmes had prepared me for what happened next. Before I had the least inkling of Holmes' intention, his pistol fired. With a shriek the wounded man spun round on us, clutching his left arm. Far from being cowed, he would, I believe, have hurled himself upon us, were it not that the sight of our weapons still leveled held him back. His face was transfigured into a satanic mask of rage and hatred, while an almost inaudible moan, I think of anger as well as pain, came from his open mouth. I heard a faint outcry from Sarah Tarlton behind me, but I did not turn.

In a matter of only a few seconds, the man who faced us had himself in hand. I had been on the point of stepping forward to do what I could for his wounded arm, from which the blood had at first flowed freely. But his whole pose was unmistakably one of menace rather than defeat, and the blood-flow ceased almost as abruptly as it had begun, so that I judged it wiser, for the moment at least, to hold my place.

But when the terrible figure spoke to Holmes, it was almost as calmly as before. "May I congratulate you on thinking of wooden bullets? I had begun to believe all Englishmen were fools."

Holmes bowed slightly, coolly accepting the compliment. Our antagonist then smiled at us, and in that moment I was very glad of the loaded weapon still in my hand.

Holmes then performed almost formal introductions, as if we were met at some afternoon social function. The Count—I now saw no reason to doubt that Holmes had discovered the killer's correct name—received Holmes' own name with utter blankness, which seemed to have a disproportionate effect upon my friend's already exhausted nerves.

"Watson," he ordered brusquely, "take Mr. Moore and Miss Tarlton outside. There are matters I must discuss in private with this man."

"Holmes," I pleaded, "let me fetch Lestrade, or Gregson."

"Very well," he answered, after a moment. "Only leave us alone, at once. Whatever happens, do not come back until I call."

Indicating to the two young Americans that they should precede me, I obeyed Holmes' order and left the room. In fact I feared to refuse, thinking that if not humored he might commit some excess even greater than deliberately wounding the unarmed man. That Holmes had deliberately shot our suspect—however desperate and potentially dangerous, still an unarmed man with his back to us—was for me the final and convincing proof that my friend's behavior was no longer adequately governed by his great powers of reason.

As soon as the three of us were out on the landing at the top of the stairs, and the door to the sitting-room closed behind us, I took Moore by the arm and whispered to him fiercely that he must commandeer the first cab in sight and take it straight to Scotland Yard. There he was to brook no delay until he had laid hold of Lestrade or Gregson—or, failing those, whatever detective was immediately available—and returned to Baker Street with the police as fast as humanly possible.

"Tell them," I concluded, "that the life and sanity of Sherlock Holmes depend upon their speed!"

He swallowed, nodded, and was gone, almost flying down the stairs.

"And is there nothing I can do?" Sarah Tarlton, a trifle pale but otherwise composed, stood anxiously beside me.

"On the contrary," I whispered urgently. "There is something you must do, while I stay here." I pulled out the scrap of paper Seward had given me and thrust it at her. "Telegraph—or telephone if you can find an instrument—to Dr. Jack Seward at that address. Say: 'Patient much worse, immediate help imperative,' and sign it 'Watson.' "

The girl very coolly repeated my instructions, took the note, and hurried off.

I turned my agonized attention again to the door at the head of the stair. The two voices within were too low for me to be able to distinguish words, but I thought I could hear the deadly strain in both of them. Indeed, there were moments when it sounded like one voice only, murmuring on and on in soft maniacal anxiety.

Not quite daring to re-enter the room against Holmes' orders, yet scarcely daring to refrain, I waited, one hand near the doorknob, the other still holding my revolver.

XIX

In stories, any number of imbeciles may be encountered, ready to deliberately insult strangers who are aiming deadly weapons at them. In real life, there are only a few folk so suicidally inclined.

"So," I said mildly, when the two men and the lovely young woman had gone out. "*You* are Sherlock Holmes." I was of course trying to give the impression of some sort of recognition—better belated than never—before a second wooden bullet should leap superbly aimed from my captor's gun, this one to splinter its way right through my vitals. His first shot, I observed, had incidentally punctured my fine trunk, as well as spraying it delicately with its owner's gore. "You must tell me," I went on, "how you managed to learn my name."

"Tut. I see by your earthen baggage that you are a foreigner, and brought your means of sustenance to England with you. The clothing and coins in it tell me what part of the world you are from. I have heard from witnesses of your accomplishments here, and have seen more evidence of them with my own eyes. Anyone who knows the slightest bit about vampires, Count, must know you by name and reputation; I might possibly have been wrong about your name, but now that I can look you in the eye, I have no doubt.''

"I am flattered. But very few breathing folk know anything of vampires. And of those few, most have the truth of the matter quite thoroughly confused with their damned superstitions. They waste good powder on silver bullets. They assault me with crucifixes, as though I were a devil and not as much a creature of the Earth, a child of God, as they are.''

"I shall not make that error.''

"I believe you. Well, what now?'' Looking about the queerly furnished room, I made a careful, empty-handed gesture. "This does not look like my idea of Scotland Yard.''

"No more am I of the official police. Nevertheless you will be well advised to answer my questions. What of Frau Grafenstein?''

"What of her?''

My foe took a half-step toward me, righteous anger rising in his voice. "Do you still think you can play games with me? I tell you I know very much—that you killed her, and that you drank her blood.'' He paused; when he went on, his voice was no longer impetuous, but inexorable. "I know, also, that no prison built can hold you for trial or execution. Therefore I stand here as your sole judge and jury—it is fortunate that there is probably no other man in England so well qualified to do so.''

I took in breath to make a sigh. "Very well—no more games.'' As I spoke I tested the fingers of my wounded arm, and was gratified to find them movable. Expected pain came with the effort, but not the wetness of fresh bleeding. As a rule we heal with great rapidity even when hurt by wood, if the damage be not immediately fatal and the weapon not held in the wound. "I killed the woman because she had attempted to kill me. Also, I was in need."

"Of—?"

"Of nourishment, of course, as well as of revenge. Is there not some old British saying, about killing two birds with one stone? I really hope that she was not a friend of yours."

"Scarcely that." He paused to study me in silence, his brows knitted with thought. There was something terribly vital he wanted to say to me—perhaps to ask—but he had not yet decided how.

I gave him half a minute, then interrupted his pregnant silence. "And how is Sally Craddock? I sent her to your police to keep her safe."

A shadow crossed Holmes' face. "I regret very much, Count, that the girl is dead."

"Ah. I should have brought her to you, instead of to the police, for safekeeping."

Holmes looked at me strangely. "The thing that drove her running, screaming, to where her enemies could reach her—was the sight of my face, Count. Or should I say, *our face?*"

"I do not understand." But then I did, even as I spoke, and suddenly much was clear to me. For example: Watson, rushing to my aid in that strange room filled with smoke and noise. And again: Matthews, in the cellar, sneering *Mr. Great Detective.*

"Ah, yes," I answered. "As you doubtless understand, I have not been permitted the luxury of mirrors for some centuries. But the resemblance is actually that close?" My foe was nodding. "So it must be. And that means that there is some . . . ah."

"Family relationship—unquestionably." We had

come to the nub of what was bothering Holmes. "What remains to be determined is its exact degree."

The aim of his revolver had never wavered in the slightest, and he had already proven his marksmanship and iron nerve; one false twitch on my part, I knew, and the great true death would greet me in that room. I may have already mentioned somewhere in these pages that I am—though not all vampires are, by any means—immune to fear, having exhausted at a tender age my whole life's allotment of that arguably useful lading. Yet honor and love of life alike forbade me to perish without a struggle.

"Mr. Holmes, my first visit to England took place but six years ago. The relationship you propose—well, doubtless it exists, since you are so certain of it. But it cannot be very close."

"The date of your first visit to England is quite irrelevant." Holmes paused again, then spoke distinctly. "My parents traveled on the Continent, in the year preceding my birth. To my certain knowledge, my mother was long unfaithful to my father; and it is equally certain that one of her paramours was of your race."

"My race, sir, is the human race."

"I think you know what I mean, Count." Holmes considered for a moment. "I have—or had; I do not know if he is still alive—a twin brother, vampire from his beginnings. You will pardon me for saying I felt an inexpressible relief on finding your trunk and thus demonstrating to my own satisfaction that you, the killer of the woman on the docks, could not be him. Since my childhood I have loathed and despised all that he stood for. All the things of the vampire world, that haunted my own early years like some—some nightmare made real. All that you are and stand for, indeed.''

"Indeed.''

"Indeed.'' And with that the vanishingly faint humor of these unplanned repetitions occurred, I think, to both of us. Not that either of us went so far as to smile, but the air had been cleared, and now something seemed to lighten in it.

"Do you mind if I sit down?'' I asked.

"Please do. But keep your hands in sight.''

I did, perching on my trunk. "I think that I begin to understand,'' I said. As a general rule, the vampire race (I still dislike that term, but there does not seem to be a better) gains members only by adoption, through initiation, rather like a hard-core political party or a religious order. A few of us, as in my own rare case, become what we are by making, as breathing human beings, a transcendent refusal to die, a truly heroic act of will. And there is one other road to the world of the *nosferatu*, which I had better digress for a moment to explain. It had been known to happen that a normally breathing woman becomes pregnant (in the traditional breathing way) while concurrently carrying on an affair with a male vampire. To such a woman, twins may be born, either fraternal or apparently identical. One of the twins in these cases is firmly committed to breathing. The other will draw air to cry with when he—or she—is spanked, but is in essence *nosferatu* from the womb.

But how, I hear a reader asking, how can hereditary characteristics such as facial appearance be passed on through love-making in the vampire style? I answer that, scientists are lately of the opinion that the whole hereditary blueprint is contained in each and every living cell of the body; that living body cells are contained in the blood; and that for a vampire's lover to drink from a vampire's veins is as traditional a part of their intercourse as is the reverse.

"Yes, Mr. Holmes, I see," I said to him. "And the year of your parents' travel on the Continent was——?"

"It was during the summer of 1853."

I cast my memory back, or tried to. After more than four centuries of life, sometimes only the very earliest and very latest events are easy to disentangle. "That was only a few months before the outbreak of the Crimean War, was it not? Of course. In my homeland, also, that was a troublous time. And where precisely did your parents travel?"

"I should prefer that you first tell me where you were that summer."

I took thought. Was he likely to accept my unsupported word? It would have been possible, perhaps, for a breathing man of genius and determination to have established something of my biography through historical research, provided he knew where to look; and so I might be caught out in a lie. (Had I known Holmes then, I would of course have replaced that "might" in my thoughts with something considerably stronger.) In any case, the situation seemed to demand a response on a higher level than routine falsehood. True, I had begun by lying to this man, in implying that I bore him no ill-will for trapping me and shooting me, but now that denial was becoming true. In fact I had already grown intensely interested in the relationship between us, and wanted to learn the truth of it, however dangerous the truth might be. If I was not the vampire lover of Holmes' mother, then surely someone closely related to me was—how else could the uncanny resemblance between us be explained?

I drew in breath for speech, and told the truth. "I went no farther west than Budapest that year. And I do not remember meeting a Mrs. Holmes at all."

A strange constellation of emotions struggled in his face for dominance. "You would remember?" The words were half a plea and half a fierce command.

She would have been a remarkable woman, I felt sure. "I am quite positive I would."

Now at last I could detect a hint of relaxation in Holmes' posture. "That year," he said, "my mother went no farther east than Switzerland." His hand holding the gun had actually begun to tremble, not with tension but with its release.

I allowed myself another smile. "Then, my dear sir, much as I would like to be able to urge some close family connection upon you now, it would appear I cannot do so." Actually, I was not at all eager to have Holmes think me a near relative. Most murders, as we know, are committed within the circle of friends and especially of family, and the man holding the gun was obviously not pleased by the thought that he and I were bound by ties of blood.

"As to our remarkable resemblance," I went on, "I can only surmise that it is the result of some distant relationship—how shall I put it?—breeding true?" And even in that moment, by the Beard of Allah even as I spoke, it came to me! My brother Radu, the one they called the Handsome in his breathing days—he *had* in fact spent a summer in Switzerland about the middle of the 19th century!

I tried to think . . . yes, that had been in 1853. But I

saw no reason to announce my recollection just at present. It meant I was Holmes' uncle, or half-uncle. Perhaps no language has a precise word for the relationship.

If his eyes had probed sharply at me before, they now pressed like twin stakes fine-pointed for bilateral impalement. "Some distant relationship, you think."

"I regret I cannot lay claim to more than that. If I remember correctly, a branch of the Draculas were drawn into the Wars of the Roses, and I am not the first of my line to set foot in England."

"Drawn in?"

"Yes. They would have come from France, I believe, in 1460, with one of the Yorkist lords—perhaps Warwick. I was myself still breathing, then. Whether any historical record still survives, I do not know. It is, as I say, a disappointment that we are not more closely tied."

"A disappointment?" He laughed, and I knew that he believed me now—because, above all else, he wanted to believe. "You will pardon my expression of relief, Count, on learning that you are not only not my twin, but cannot possibly be the man responsible for his existence."

I nodded, looking gravely sympathetic.

Holmes pressed on, pouring out words that he had probably spoken to no other living being, and would probably never speak again. "I have not seen my twin since we were children. I intend never again to speak his name, and it would not pain me to learn that he is dead—certainly and finally dead. It is because of him that my father went early to his grave—because of him and because of my mother, who went to her grave even sooner—went to it, *but not to stay*. There followed years of hell, ending only when my father and my older brother, with their own hands . . . do you understand me? Hell ended for us only when her death had become final and absolute. Well, I hate her no longer." Holmes spoke these last words as if surprised by them himself.

He paused, he shook his head, and I saw that in a moment he had forced from his mind the horrors—as he saw them—of his early life. It is, although I did not say so to him, a family trait that one is able to control one's own thoughts so ruthlessly and so well.

"But all of this," Holmes went on urgently, "even this, is at the moment of very little importance. Count Dracula, your life and mine are small things compared to what is now at stake."

I looked at him closely. But no, he was still in too solemn a mood to perpetrate a pun consciously.

"I do not understand," I said.

"I refer to the fate of London itself. In a moment I shall explain." His weapon's aim was perfectly steady again. "If, Count Dracula—if, I say—I were to permit you to walk from this room a free man, what would your next move be?"

"I have some business in London still unfinished. When that is done I shall be peaceably on my way."

"And the nature of this business?"

"Personal." I smiled yet again, liking the way this man —my nephew, or whatever he might be— met my eye. The more we talked, the more I knew him as a true Dracula. "But then, I suppose it is public, too. Your great city will be a better place when it is done."

"Jem Matthews was of course a part of the same business. As was the lady on the dock."

"Two parts now concluded. But there are at least two more to be finished before honor will allow me to return to private life and cease to trouble your police. And now, my dear Mr. Holmes, I think that I must bid you adieu.''

"Ah?"

"Your friend Watson has gone for the redoubtable Lestrade, or Gregson, who are strangers to me, but whose profession I can readily enough guess. A van-load of police are surely on their way here by now. I will allow another minute or two in which to finish this very interesting talk; but then I mean to take my trunk, which you have so kindly found for me, and go on my way. Are you prepared to try to shoot me as I do?''

XX

Though my vigil at the head of the stair seemed endless, actually no more than a few minutes could have passed before there came a rush of metal-rimmed wheels against the curb below, and the sound of several pairs of feet alighting on the pavement. I went down as quickly and quietly as possible, and met a police constable and two burly men in civilian clothing, just ready to ring. Getting out of the carriage behind these men was Jack Seward, who gripped my arm.

"Where is he?" Seward demanded.

"Upstairs. Thank God you have come so soon."

"Fortunately I was already in the city, and happened to communicate by telephone with the asylum, where they had just received your message." Seward folded his spectacles and slipped them into a pocket, readying himself for action. "From the tone of your message, Watson, there is not a moment to lose. Lead the way, quickly!"

We had no more than set foot upon the stairs when a shot rang out. I ran on up, and without ceremony flung open the sitting-room door, which had not been locked. Holmes sat slumped in a chair in the middle of the room, one hand holding his revolver hanging almost limply at his side, the other hand raised to his face. He was quite alone. There was some disorder evident, in the way of rugs and furniture being disarranged, and even in that first glance I noted that the great trunk was gone. Beyond the motionless figure in the chair, the door to Holmes' bedroom stood open, and through the doorway I glimpsed a window raised, with curtains blowing in the morning breeze.

As we burst in, Holmes raised his eyes, to scowl at the rush of men.

"Where is the prisoner?" I exclaimed.

"Escaped," he answered shortly. Before he could say more, one of the burly civilian attendants had him by each arm, and the revolver had been wrenched roughly from his hand. Seward, springing past me, took only an instant to force up the sleeve of Holmes' dressing-gown, and to plunge the needle of a hypodermic into his arm. My friend, who had begun to struggle, in another moment sank back limp and helpless.

My anger blazed up. "You have no justification for such treatment!" I protested, and moved forward to clutch Seward by the arm. To my utter amazement, I immediately felt my own arms pinioned from behind. Looking over my shoulder, I saw it was the uniformed man who had grabbed me. I opened my mouth for another protest, and tried to pull free; but the two men who had been holding Holmes now released his inert form and came to lay their hands on me as well. Their leader still brandished his hypodermic, and as one of his confederates pushed up the sleeve of my right arm, he pressed it home. The last thing I saw before lapsing into unconsciousness was a smile of evil triumph disfiguring Jack Seward's handsome face.

My return to awareness was a slow and painful

process, marred again and again by irresistible relapses into drugged sleep, a sleep shot through with strange dreams or visions. At one point it seemed to me that I was manacled helplessly to a peculiar cart or bed. Again, the comely face of a young woman in a high-collared gown, a complete stranger to me, was hovering near; and I thought she exchanged words with some unseen personage just outside my range of vision. As she gazed at me the young woman seemed concerned about my plight, though she was evidently unwilling or unable to take any helpful action.

When at last I fully recovered my senses, there was no woman to be seen. To my dismay, however, the metal cart and the shackles holding me to it proved to be only too horribly real. I was held down on my back, unable to do much more than turn my head, in a small room that was more like a cell than a bedchamber. It was sparsely furnished, and the paint on the walls was old and worn. Through shutters and bars, a sectioned shaft of wan, orange-yellow sunlight entered the sole window almost horizontally, suggesting that the day was nearly spent. The effects of the drug had evidently lasted many hours.

On turning my head I was shocked to discover a still figure similarly bound to another cart, not five feet from my own. I leave it to the reader to imagine my sensations on recognizing in the dim light the face of Sherlock Holmes, pale and motionless as death.

I whispered his name repeatedly, each time louder than the last, but he made not the least response; and I had about decided to see what I could accomplish in the way of obtaining help by using my lungs at their loudest, when a key rattled sharply in the lock of the stout door that formed the only entrance to the room. It opened, and Seward came in, a small lighted lamp in hand.

"What does this mean?" I demanded of him, in quiet rage.

He seemed not to hear, but closed the door behind him, then put on his spectacles and came forward, holding up his lamp. He bent over the inert form on the cart beside mine, and looked for a long moment before he straightened up.

"Incredible!" Seward muttered then, as if speaking only to himself. "An amazing likeness to the Count— yes, now I see."

"You know Count Dracula?" I asked—rather stupidly, I am afraid. It may have been that the last traces of the injected drug were still affecting my brain.

He turned to me with a short, unpleasant laugh. "Oh yes, Watson—Dracula and I are old acquaintances, though I had thought him six years dead. What can you tell me of how he came to be involved in this?"

I could not have given the villain a helpful answer had I wanted to; but rather than even give the appearance of cooperation, I simply pressed my lips together.

He shook his head, as if at an obstinate patient. "You are mistaken, if you imagine you will be able to withold information from me. There are some things I mean to learn, from Holmes or from you; and the sooner I learn them, the less painful your remaining hours will be." He looked at me, shrugged, and drew from a pocket of his coat a small case of surgical instruments, such as any doctor might carry about with him. When the case snapped open in his hand, the gleaming knives and scissors, all familiar tools of my own trade, appeared to me in a light in which I had never before seen them.

Seward's hand was hovering over the open case, as if doubtful which bright implement to choose, when there came a sudden bold rattle at the door. From just outside, a woman's voice, young and carefree, called out: "Jack? I say, are you in there?"

Muttering something under his breath, Seward snapped shut the case again and replaced it in his pocket. Going to the door, he unbolted it and opened it very slightly. "Mina," he remonstrated calmly, "I am afraid that there are patients here."

Through the partially open door I could catch just a glimpse of a young woman's face in the brighter hallway outside. It was the very face that I had seen, and taken for part of a dream, while I was still half-conscious.

Now she replied lightly: "Oh, I am so dreadfully sorry, Jack. You look somewhat harried; is there anything that Jonathan or I can do?"

"No, nothing, thanks. I have my attendants on call."

"I met one just now." She lowered her voice. "A rather brutal-looking fellow, who scowled at me when I came down this way from upstairs."

"I shall speak to him. However, I am afraid I am not as free of professional matters as I had hoped to be."

"But two patients in one room? Isn't that odd?" Now she was trying boldly to peer in past his shoulder.

"Help!" I croaked, loud as I could through my parched throat, thinking that I should never get a better chance. "Send for the police!"

Seward, not in the least perturbed, went on without even looking back in my direction. "Unusual, yes. But don't worry your pretty head, my dear. What the

French call *folie a deux*, meaning two patients with a shared delusion. Just for the present I don't want to separate them."

"Police!" I repeated hoarsely. "Tell them Sherlock Holmes is held a prisoner here!"

The young lady giggled, as I continued my cries and groans for help.

Continued Seward: "As you perceive, things may get just a bit noisy here before we are finished. Don't let it bother you; and you might just say a word to Jonathan when you go up, so he won't be perturbed if there are a few yells. As soon as I am able I'll join you—for dinner, I hope."

"I'll mention it to him." To my despair I heard her voice begin to fade as she turned away. "But you know Jonathan—nothing perturbs him, or at least nothing has for the past six years." She started to leave, then turned back. "By the way, I suppose you have no objection to my using your telephone? I wanted to call Arthur and tell him Jonathan and I and the children will be with you tomorrow for the procession. I hope His Lordship has enough seats available."

"I'm sure he has—but by all means, call him if you like. And—Mina? Before you go. The—the other night I spoke too quickly. But it was the strength of my feelings that led me—"

The young woman's voice grew steely. "I told you, Jack, that if you spoke that way to me again, you should regret it. There is one man whom I love, above all others. And you are not him." In the next moment she was gone.

Seward, with the bitter smile of his parting from the lady still on his face, turned back to me, leaving the door ajar. It was a moment before he spoke. "Would you like to try calling for the police again, Watson? As you see, it will avail you absolutely nothing.''

In a moment, a hulking attendant had appeared silently at the door; I recognized him as the ''constable'' who had assisted at our abduction, though he had since changed out of his uniform. At Seward's order our two carts, Holmes' first and mine following, were wheeled out of the room and across the adjoining corridor. The brief look afforded by this passage convinced me that the building was, or had been, an asylum or hospital of some sort; and the deadly silence of the place indicated we were somewhere outside of London.

On the other side of the corridor we were wheeled into a somewhat larger chamber, Seward closing and locking the door when we were all in. As we entered, a strange smell assailed my nostrils. At first I thought of open drains, but there was in this stench a peculiar muskiness that quickly brought to mind the idea of an unclean zoo.

When Seward brought his lamp into the room I saw the animal responsible, and at first could not believe my eyes. Crouched in a metal cage against the farther wall was a creature bigger than a large hound, yet unmistakably a rodent. Its feral eyes gleamed redly at me in the lamplight, and its snout twitched, before it turned away to pace its cage, on feet repulsively naked-looking below the matted fur covering its legs.

Averting my gaze from this disgusting sight, I saw with mixed sensations that Holmes' eyelids were now open. His eyes looked flat and lifeless, and they wandered aimlessly, showing the continuing effects of the drug Seward had injected, rather than any understanding of our predicament.

Seward set down his lamp upon a table, and now,

also seeing that Holmes was awake, came over to offer a light bow. "Mr. Holmes. I am very glad to meet you—I was about to say, even under these unhappy circumstances. But then, from my point of view, it would be easy enough to imagine our meeting under circumstances infinitely worse."

Holmes' eyes moved dreamily to focus on the face which hovered over him. His lips formed a word, scarcely audible: "Who—?"

Seward smiled again. "You may call me Jack. Why not? We are about to establish a very intimate relationship—unless you, Dr. Watson, are ready now to begin to talk to me? No? Too bad."

Our captor walked over to the cage, and there turned back to face us. "Would it surprise you gentlemen to learn that a large part of this animal's diet is human flesh? Poor Scott, when he caught the beast, was having a difficult time providing its accustomed fare . . . not a lot of plague victims around just then. As usual, those of us who scrupled less accomplished more—as soon as we had taken over his camp, Scott himself went along the path that you may take. He went rather quickly, however, whereas you will not . . . and all for the lack of a few words."

He paused, looking from one of us to the other. "Well, Mr. Holmes? Come, no need to look so dazed, I know you are awake now. Have you nothing to tell us yet about your work and Scotland Yard's? For example, where have you been looking for my infected rats? Ah, it is too bad you do not answer, for it means that I must begin to feed Dr. Watson here to the Rat. Campbell, come here and remove the doctor's shoes. Feet first will be best; that way good old Watson will remain able to join in our conversation. We shall have all night to discuss my questions; my departure for France will not take place until dawn.''

Another of the burly attendants had now come into the room, and with the one already present started to take off my boots. Looking down past my own feet, I could see the slavering animal pacing in its cage.

Holmes' voice, in the form of an unrecognizable croak, now issued at last from his parched lips. "Why not . . . to the fleas?''

Seward frowned; evidently this particular reaction was not one he had anticipated. "But my dear sir, surely you realize that the time for experiments with fleas is past? . . . I see, you pretend ignorance so I shall think it a waste of time to question you. No, Holmes, that is a rather pathetic effort, and it won't do; I have too much respect for your powers. You must realize that by now I have obtained my thousand rats and they are ready, filled with plague from this my walking reservoir.'' He tapped on the bars of the cage, and the creature within bared its yellow teeth and strained against the barrier on my side. Its eyes were fixed on my bound and helpless figure, as if it were used to this procedure, and knew what to expect next.

Seward went on: "Before we depart for France we shall launch my thousand rats into the London sewers, where in a day or two they will begin to sicken and die. In a week a million rats will be infected, and in a week after that, possibly a million men, women, and children. A pity you and the damned bloodsucker did not allow us a chance, here in London, to arrange a fool-proof system for collecting our ransom—but in the next city the authorities will be not at all stiff-necked about paying; not with the example of the world's greatest metropolis fresh before them. *You'll* be in no position to interfere, next time, and if Dracula continues to take an interest I'll find a way to deal with him—perhaps he would not refuse a partnership.''

He was interrupted by a rattle at the door, which in the next moment was unlocked from outside. It swung open to admit the man Holmes had already identified as Dr. David Fitzroy. Fitzroy's mustache had been shaved off, and a pair of sideburns were under cultivation since I had seen him at Barley's, but still I had no difficulty in recognizing him again.

Exchanging terse greetings with Seward, he crossed the room to draw a blind over the window—the last faint rays of the sun were just disappearing there, and my heart sank at the thought that I should probably never see it again. Coming back, Fitzroy cast a single, impersonal glance at me, then paused to look down at my companion. ''So,'' he murmured, ''this is what the greatest detective in London looks like. But you know, I have the feeling that I've seen him before.''

Seward at once changed the subject. ''You have the extra serum with you? Just in case any of us should need a dose?''

''Yes—there are only six of us left now, I believe? I saw Day and Morley upstairs, and here are Campbell and the Pincher.''

''That's right.''

''Then there's plenty.'' And Fitzroy indicated a small black bag he had brought in with him and set down on the table. The two muscular attendants, who had been following this portion of the conversation with special interest, now nodded with satisfaction. They had completed the task of removing my boots, and were standing one on each side of my cart, ready to push it up to the cage when their masters should command them.

I thought Seward was on the point of giving that command, but Fitzroy held him for a moment with a gesture. "We're all ready for departure, then. The other cage for the Rat is aboard the launch, and the launch is fueled and ready. We'll just stop at the old place to release the rats into the sewers, and then be on our way for France. But what about—?" And he motioned toward the upstairs.

"My guests? What about them?" Seward asked cooly.

"Well, the other day you mentioned the possibility of one more person coming with us, and I saw you talking to the woman then, and I thought . . ."

Seward turned away. "No, I care nothing about her. Let her stay and enjoy the plague with the rest of London."

Just at this point, I was startled by a low moaning or keening sound, proceeding from the still figure lying at my side. When I looked toward Holmes, his dazed expression had not altered, though his eyes were now fixed on Seward. The strange wail issued from my companion in a way that made my hair start to rise on end—then it cut off abruptly, and he muttered a few words that I could not make out.

Seward and Fitzroy both hurried to his cart, where they bent over him on either side, straining to hear better. But hardly had they done so, when Seward abruptly straightened again. Following the direction of his suddenly staring eyes, I saw with blank incomprehension that Holmes' right arm had somehow come free of its shackle—the steel ring was still closed, and fixed to the cart, but it no longer held his wrist.

Frowning, Seward reached to take hold of the escaped limb. But that thin, white hand rose steadily on its lean arm. It brushed aside Seward's grasping fists as though they were those of an infant, and took him neatly by the throat.

Simultaneously Fitzroy straightened up, as if he realized that something had gone wrong but was not yet clear on what. Before he could do anything purposeful, the left hand of the figure on the cot slid easily of its restraint, and struck at him with a cobra's speed. I saw its fingers clench round the unfortunate Fitzroy's neck. His eyes started from their sockets, as bone and muscle together were crumpled like twists of paper in that grip. An instant later, and his lifeless body had been flung aside, like some huge, weightless doll.

So quickly was the incredible deed accomplished that it was over before the attendants had been sufficiently aroused from their inattention to throw themselves into the struggle. Meanwhile I, on my own cart, strove with might and main—but uselessly—to free myself.

The cart beside mine slid and rolled, then went over with a crash upon its side. All four of his limbs now freed as if by magic, the man who had been on it stood erect. He was red-eyed and terrible of visage as he fought, and to my dying day I shall hear the droning shriek of rage that issued from his lips.

Though his two new opponents bulked huge on either side, they could not stand against him—this, despite the fact that his right hand constantly maintained its grip on Seward's neck and collar. First one and then the other of the burly henchmen was shaken like a rat in the grip of a terrier, then hurled aside. The body of the first struck the door of the room with an impact that made the solid oak tremble, then slid down into a lifeless heap. The second man, an instant later, was thrown against the cage with such force that the iron structure tilted on its base. From my own helpless position, I saw with horror how the animal inside rushed in mad excitement against its bars. It reached out its muzzle far enough to sink fangs into the shoulder of the last man to fall. He was still living, for now his scream went up and up.

The Count—for by now I realized that despite dark hair, shaven eyebrows, and certain other facial alterations, it must be he—now stood alone, silent but expressing in his demonic grimace the triumph that he evidently felt. His chief and final victim was still in his grasp—still in his grasp and living, for his grip on Seward's throat had not yet exerted deadly power.

Jack Seward hung in that lean and terrible hand as helpless as a kitten. He kicked and writhed in desperation, and his arms beat uselessly against the arm of steel that held him. The pressure of the Count's thumb on Seward's jaw had twisted his head round until his neck must have been on the point of snapping, and his face grew purple with congested blood. In this state Seward fastened his wretched gaze on me. As if he no longer realized that I was bound and helpless, he choked out an appeal:

"Watson . . . help . . . he's not human . . ."

Perhaps Seward had a moment to read my bitter answer in my face, before Dracula's resistless one-handed grip spun him away and dragged him toward the cage. A last desperate kick of the victim's foot happened to strike my cart, and turned it so I could no longer see what was going on. I heard a rattle, as of one of the cage's small doors being opened—as it would have opened for me had Seward's own plan been carried out. Then I would have stopped my ears had I been able to, so terrible were the screams that began.

These awful outcries soon subsided, though not entirely. The room seemed to be spinning around me, and there was a roaring in my ears. And now it seemed to me that I once more heard the woman's voice, this time entreating: "Vlad—Vlad, stop it, please. I do not care what he has done—"

"For you, my dear," came a low reply, and with that the last horrible cry cut off abruptly. "There are still two more upstairs?"

"Yes. Only menials. And what of *him?*" asked the woman, her voice sounding shaken. "Will you not loose him from that cart?"

"Hush, my darling! He will hear you. He must not know that you and I are lovers."

"Dr. Watson is a gentleman who minds his own affairs, I am sure. You must free him."

"Very well, but later. First I must see about the two upstairs." The two voices faded completely as the door squeaked once more.

I was left alone in that room of death, where all was silence, save for one hideous sound somewhere behind me—the frantic snuffling of the caged Rat. But no, there was another still alive. I heard a faint human groan. It was repeated.

By dint of great straining I extended the shoeless toes of one foot far enough to reach the wall, and managed to push hard enough to turn my cart. At once I saw that Seward himself must be dead; his horribly mangled body lay half in and half out of the cage, blocking the small door which had been opened for feeding purposes. The angle that his head made with his trunk showed that his neck must have been completely broken at the last.

A shape stirred on the floor just outside the cage, and I saw that one of the brutal attendants was not yet dead. With many groans, struggling against what must have been massive internal injuries, the man called Campbell dragged himself to his feet. It was an effort that could not be sustained. Even as an uproar—a muffled cry, a shot, the sound of running feet—broke out somewhere overhead, Campbell staggered again, lurched against the table where the oil lamp stood, and carried both over in his last collapse. Flames sprang up to lick at the fallen table, at the wall, and at the cage itself.

Under the stimulus of fire, the caged beast, whether by instinct or crude intelligence, pulled entirely into the cage the body it had already begun to devour. Through the small doorway thus left unobstructed, it strove desperately to force itself to freedom.

I shouted until I thought my voice must fail, yet heard no answer. The uproar continued upstairs, with more shots, and trampling feet, and confused cries. When at last I thought I heard an answering yell in response to one of mine, I took heart and continued my efforts to be heard.

Meanwhile, to my horror, the Rat was succeeding in forcing its body through the aperture, which had at first seemed much too small. Squeezing its body inch by inch past the constricting metal, it bared its teeth at me—my cart lay now between it and the door. With a last effort, it burst free, and crouched to spring upon me.

A revolver shot rang out, near at hand, and the brute

fell dead into the spreading flames. "Watson!" cried a familiar voice. "Thank God!" A face loomed over me, coughing in the smoke, and altered by false bushy eyebrows, but still beyond all doubt the face of Sherlock Holmes.

Though volunteers from the nearest houses soon came to fight the fire, it had gained too great a start to be controlled before it had destroyed the entire building. The gray light of dawn found me wrapped in a blanket donated by some kindly neighbor, and seated on a stump in the half-wooded grounds of the old asylum while I contemplated the smoldering wreckage.

With the exception of some trifling burns, I was uninjured. So were Holmes and Lestrade, who had searched the building for me at considerable danger to themselves, after besting Seward's two remaining henchmen in a deadly struggle on the floor above. My friends had then carried me out of the building, cart and all, to a spot far enough removed from the blaze for Holmes to take the time to pick the locks that shackled me.

Nor had any of the Harker family, Seward's guests, been hurt. All of them were dressed as if they had been hastily aroused, and were the picture of innocence and shock—Mrs. Harker, the young woman I had already seen and heard; her husband Jonathan, a rather pudgy man of about forty, prematurely white-haired; and their two small children with a young governess. Mrs. Harker, so she said, had chanced to be awake, and had smelled smoke, thus giving her entire family a chance to get safely to the open air. In the presence of the folk from neighboring villas and houses, she said not a word—nor did Holmes or Lestrade—of shots or fighting or indeed anything out of the ordinary beyond the fire itself.

The blaze was blamed for the extermination of most of the staff of the institution, of which only an innocent cook and stableboy appeared to have survived—and for the death of Dr. Fitzroy, who, it seemed, had been visiting in connection with some animal experiments. In these, it appeared, I also had been taking part, and I was the sole survivor of those who had done so. Lestrade, who of course had at least some idea of the true state of affairs, hastened to assure other police arriving on the scene that I would give a statement in due time, but was in no condition to be questioned just at present.

Right after the police came Lord Godalming, in his own carriage, to exchange shocked words with his old friends the Harkers, and then with Holmes and Lestrade.

Then he came, shaking his head, to where I sat upon my stump. "Dr. Watson," he muttered, "very fortunate that you could get out alive. They tell me there were five dead in all, including poor Jack."

"Six," corrected Lestrade. "We found one chap just over there at the edge of the trees. He was running for help, I should guess, and in his panic evidently fell and broke his neck . . . a bad business, very bad."

I shivered slightly, thinking the broken neck not at all likely to have been an accident. But for the time being I said nothing.

"Very bad," His Lordship agreed, distractedly. "Watson, I suppose you have met the Harkers?"

I was thereupon introduced properly to the husband; the wife smiled gallantly and said: "Dr. Watson and I did meet last night, though we scarcely had a chance to speak to each other—the men were so busy with their work. I did mean to come back, Doctor." These words she spoke very earnestly. "But I was delayed."

"I do appreciate the thought," I murmured. My eye at this moment chanced to fall upon the Harker children; they were a boy and a girl, and as I now saw, undoubtedly twins. When the girl looked at me I thought I saw in her face something wild and savage—a passing shade that I never should have recognized before I had met the Count. It may have been my imagination, for the strange look was gone in a moment, leaving only a child who regarded me thoughtfully.

At this point we were distracted by another arrival, that of Peter Moore and Sarah Tarlton, who held hands as they dismounted from a hansom and approached us. Word of the fire had reached them through the police, as I discovered later. I saw Miss Tarlton pale at the sickening smell of death-by-fire that hovered over the still-smoldering ruins. Holmes broke off a whispered conversation with Lestrade to greet them.

"I must report that my investigations have had an unhappy conclusion as regards the object of your search," my friend informed her. "There is no longer any doubt that John Scott perished in the South Seas."

His words were painful to the girl, but it was obvious that she no longer found them in the least surprising. She raised her chin. "And was his death a natural one?"

"I fear that it was not. But you have my solemn word, for whatever comfort it may provide, that those responsible have already paid the full penalty for their crime."

A few minutes later Holmes and I were on our way back to Baker Street. It was, as I well remember, June

22, the day of Her Majesty's Jubilee procession. Somewhere musicians had risen early to begin their final practice, and from the distance, strains of martial music drifted to our ears. Though traffic was already snarled in places, the whole metropolis was in a festive mood, for which its people had even better reason than they knew.

We had continued our progress for some distance into the increasingly busy streets before I broke a silence by remarking:

"He is not dead, you know."

"He?"

"Holmes . . . do not play games."

My friend gave the ghost of a chuckle. "I do not doubt for a moment that the Count still lives. When he and I came to our agreement, it was not part of the plan that he should die."

"Only that you should switch identities for a time. Well, the plan succeeded, though I never should have trusted him." Then I bit my lip, recalling whom I had chosen to trust.

"Whatever else he may be, Watson, Count Dracula is a man of honor—a rarity in this day and age, and perhaps in any. We had a strong common ground in our enemies; once I had made sure of that, I knew the gamble was worthwhile. Dracula, his eyebrows and hair trimmed and darkened, and with a few other touches from my make-up box, remained in our apartment wearing my clothing, to let himself be kidnapped and taken to the enemy headquarters, where the men he yearned to destroy were most likely to come within his grasp."

I shuddered.

"I shall lose no sleep over their fate, Watson, whatever it may have been. But I confess that I never expected you to be taken with him, and I had a bad moment or two when I learned of your abduction. The Count was willing to gamble that the means of kidnapping would do him no serious harm; it was a much longer chance that you took so unknowingly. I was much relieved when Mrs. Harker's guarded telephone message came to me, through the police, telling me that you were at least still alive."

"Ah. But how did you know that our chief enemy was Seward? And that when he came to our rooms it would be to kidnap you rather than to kill you outright?"

"My dear Watson, the next time you attempt to drug one of your patients with curried chicken, it would be well to choose a subject not yet out of his first childhood, or else far gone into his second."

"Holmes, I—"

He waved me to silence. "I was not certain whether this move was your own idea, or—you have never done anything of the kind before—whether it might have been suggested by some seeming friend with an ulterior motive. I pretended to sleep late, but was nevertheless up in good time to eavesdrop on your entire conversation in our rooms with Dr. Seward and Lord Godalming. This gave me no reason to suspect the latter, but it strongly aroused my suspicions against Seward. When I came out into the sitting-room later, I took the liberty of stumbling against you in my bemused state, and emptied your pocket—I know in which one you always carry pills—of Seward's gift. A little chemical analysis, and I was certain of my foe, though I still had not a shred of evidence against him save for the pill itself. The drug was an East Indian one, unlikely to be fatal but producing a violent temporary madness. Sir Jasper Meek confirmed my findings. You were meant to give it to me, then call in Seward for more help. He would thus be enabled to interrogate me at his leisure in his stronghold at Purfleet. Now I knew he did not intend to kill me outright. I replaced the pill with a harmless substitute, put the box back into your pocket . . . "

"Holmes, I must apologize."

"It is not at all necessary. If your plan unintentionally endangered my life, so did mine accidentally place yours in peril."

"How did you work out your plan with Dracula?"

"Well, he and I pushed his great box up onto the roof, out of sight, so he might appear to have taken it away. We disarranged the sitting-room to suggest struggle or flight. Then, while I was busy with our disguises, the Count had time to tell me where the enemy had formerly kept their headquarters. Leaving him dressed in some of my clothing, I went out through our old second exit, that served us so well, as you must recall, in the recovery of the Mazarin Stone. I was thus free to take effective action in the field, against an enemy who thought me safely out of his way.

"Once I had found the abandoned building described to me by the Count, and entered it, inspection soon convinced me that the abandonment could be no more than temporary. In particular, I had been intrigued by Dracula's mention of rats that he heard there on his second visit. Now, men experimenting with transmission of plague by means of rats would hardly have allowed their laboratories to be so casually infested.

"I searched, and on a lower level, which the Count had not bothered to look at, I found hundreds of brown and black rats caged. Food and water had been provided for them, yet there was evidence of sickness, and I did not go too close. I hastened instead to enlist the help of Sir Jasper, and the faithful Lestrade. I am happy to report that the cages and their contents were drenched in carbolic and incinerated, shortly after being inspected for the last time by one of their owners, the late Dr. Fitzroy. Lestrade and I followed him back to Purfleet, while he thought himself secure."

For a while we both were silent, as our cab labored forward in the morning traffic. Then stubbornly I came back to my subject.

"I admit, Holmes, that I may owe the Count my life. But I think he would as cheerfully have killed me, had I stood in his way. Holmes, the man is still at large, and he—he is a vampire."

"Ha! You saw enough, did you, to convince yourself of that? Perhaps someday I shall ask to hear all the details." Holmes folded his arms and sat back, softly whistling something from a French opera. His manner was, it seemed to me, very strangely altered from that of recent days; he could now speak lightly, almost frivolously, of this being whose mere existence had seemed likely to drive him mad.

I began another protest, which he interrupted. "So, Watson, you are now convinced. Would you like to try to convince Lestrade? Besides, with what real wrongdoing can we charge the Count? In conscience, Watson. I do not speak strictly of the law."

I could not immediately find an answer that adequately expressed my deep forebodings, and in a moment Holmes went on. "It has long been my practice, as you know, to bend the law for special cases. If I could do so for Von Herder, how much more for the man who has, more than anyone else, saved London?

In fact, I should like to reassure the Count that, insofar as the matter rests with me, he and his kind will be subjected to no probing and no publicity.''

"To reassure him? But how are we to communicate with this man at all?''

"Your gallantry does you credit, Watson. I myself heard enough from Madam Harker, and saw enough, to convince me that you cannot be ignorant of her status vis-a-vis the Count. But to use that road would show a certain lack of artistry on our part, and perhaps a certain indelicacy as well. We must be subtle, Watson . . . . I think some statement to the effect that vampires are unheard of in English criminal practice, worked into one of your little tales—the tale in this case made up out of whole cloth—would serve the purpose admirably. What would you say to something like *The Sussex Vampire* as a title?''

"I would say that any story involving Sherlock Holmes, the art of ratiocination, *and* vampires, cannot fail to appear more than a little preposterous.''

"Oh, I quite agree, Watson, I quite agree. But then, my dear Watson, so does life.''

THE BEST IN HORROR

FRED SABERHAGEN

THE TOR DOUBLES

Two complete short science fiction novels in one volume!